Lara is a country parson's daughter, eager for adventure, who trades places with a friend so she can experience first-hand the lives of the very rich. At the lavish estate of the Marquis of Keyston, masquerading as a governess, she learns an unexpected lesson in love—in the arms of her employer!

THE POOR GOVERNESS

The First
Camfield Romance!

Camfield Place,
Hatfield,
Hertfordshire,
England

Dearest Reader,

This is a new and exciting concept of Jove, who are bringing out my new novels under the name of Camfield Romances.

Camfield Place is my home in Hertfordshire, England, which originally existed in 1275, but was rebuilt in 1867 by the grandfather of Beatrix Potter.

It was here in this lovely house, with the best view in Hertfordshire, that she wrote *The Tale of Peter Rabbit*. Mr. McGregor's garden is exactly as she described it. The door in the wall that the fat little rabbit could not squeeze underneath and the goldfish pool where the white cat sat twitching its tail are still there.

I had Camfield Place blessed when I came here in 1950 and was so happy with my husband until he died, and now with my children and grandchildren, that I know that the atmosphere is filled with love and we have all been very lucky.

It is easy here to write of love and that is why I feel you will enjoy the new Camfield Romances which come to you with *my love*.

Bless you,

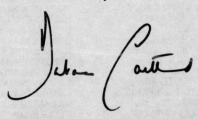

A Camfield Romance by

BARBARA CARTLAND

THE POOR GOVERNESS

A JOVE BOOK

THE POOR GOVERNESS

A Jove Book / published by arrangement with
the author

PRINTING HISTORY
Jove edition / February 1982

ISBN: 0-515-06293-6

PRINTED IN THE UNITED STATES OF AMERICA

author's note

The Governess's lot in the Victorian and Edwardian eras was often miserable and frightening as I have described in this novel. My mother always said she was so sorry for them, as if they talked they were considered 'forward' and if they were silent, 'dull.'

A pretty Governess was also too often considered fair game and I remember hearing a well known 'Dasher' of my mother's generation saying:

"There was a jolly pretty Governess in one house I visited. I was considering seducing her but thought it unfair. Then damn-me I learnt my best friend had got there first."

Between upstairs and downstairs, and often ignored by both, a Governess was lonely and isolated. But there was no other career open to respectable young women at that time except to be a companion to an old and usually disagreeable Dowager.

THE POOR GOVERNESS

chapter one

1877

THE door opened, and a voice said sharply:

"Come along, Miss Lara, it's a nice day, and you should be out getting the air instead of being cooped up here scribbling your head off!"

The Honourable Lara Hurley raised her face to say laughingly:

"I am scribbling my head off to some purpose, Nanny, and when I am famous you will be proud of me."

Nanny, who had been with the family for over twenty years, merely snorted disparagingly, and coming into the room picked up a scarf that was on one chair, a sun-bonnet on another, and several books which had been thrown onto the floor.

Lara sat back in her chair and exclaimed:

"Oh, Nanny, now you have broken the thread of

what I was going to say, and I am having such trouble with this chapter anyway."

"Why you should want to write a book when the house is full of them already, is beyond my comprehension," Nanny replied.

"You say that now, but when it is published you will be the first person who will want me to sign a copy for you."

Nanny sniffed as if that was very unlikely and Lara went on:

"It is all very well, Nanny, but what else can I do to make money? And as you well know, we need it!"

"It's not the sort of occupation that will bring in much money," Nanny replied. "From all I've heard, famous authors have always starved in garrets before they got their books published."

"You are quite right," Lara said, "and although I am not starving, thanks to you, I am desperately in need of a new gown, and if I have to go to Church in the same bonnet for another five years, I am sure it will fall to pieces while I am singing the psalms, and you will really be ashamed of me!"

Nanny did not reply and Lara went on:

"Not that there is anybody in the Church who would notice what I am wearing! And seeing how dull and uneventful this village is, is it surprising that I have to use my imagination to find excitement?"

"I'm not going to say you shouldn't use your imagination, Miss Lara," Nanny said tartly, "but you look pale, and it's fresh air you need to put the roses back in your cheeks, and I can't think why you don't take up gardening or sketching, as other young ladies do."

"Which young ladies?" Lara enquired. "There are none of my age around here, as you are well aware."

Because she thought she was getting the worst of the argument, Nanny walked to the door.

"I can't stay here gossiping all day, Miss Lara," she said. "I've got your father's dinner to prepare and the so-called chicken old Jacobs has killed is so tough it'll have to be boiled for hours before you can get your teeth into it!"

Nanny did not wait for a reply, but went from the Study shutting the door behind her, and therefore did not hear Lara laugh.

The toughness of the chickens was an everlasting bone of contention between Nanny and the odd-job man who stoked the boiler, planted the vegetables in the garden, and cleaned out the stables.

Lara often wondered what they would do without him, for she was quite certain they would find no one else who would do what Jacobs did for so small a wage.

'Money! Money!' she thought to herself now. 'It is not the "root of all evil," it is the cause of all discomfort and worry!'

It seemed ridiculous, she often thought, that her father had come into the family title but with not a penny to go with it.

As the younger son of the third Lord Hurlington he had gone into the Church while his older brother, Edward, as was traditional, had served in the Grenadier Guards which was the family Regiment.

When Edward died in Egypt, not of wounds but of sandfly fever, the Reverend Arthur Hurlington had become the heir to the Barony.

But when Lara's grandfather had died he had left a mass of debts which were only partially cleared by the sale of a family house and its contents.

Because he was conscientious and also honourable, the new Lord Hurlington worked valiantly trying to pay off the debts that remained out of his very small stipend.

This meant that his wife and daughter had to pinch and save every penny, and such things as a new gown or even a new bonnet were all expected to wait until in some far distant future the family were clear of the millstone round their necks.

"How could Grandpapa have been so extravagant?" Lara had asked her mother a dozen times.

Lady Hurlington not only had no answer, but a year ago had seemed to relinquish her hold on life, and it seemed she just faded away.

Lara bitterly blamed the fact that there was not sufficient food to sustain her, nor could they afford the expensive medicines she obviously needed.

Since she had become eighteen and no longer considered herself a school-girl, she had been obsessed by the idea of earning money.

At the same time, she knew it would be impossible for her to leave her father alone, even if she were offered lucrative employment elsewhere.

Actually there was no chance of that.

The only careers open to young women who were ladies were either to be a companion to some cantankerous old Dowager, or else to become a Governess.

"You're certainly too young to be that," Nanny said when Lara talked to her about it.

"I have also no wish to teach children anyway," Lara said, "and Mama always said a Governess lived a miserable life somewhere between Heaven and Hell!"

Nanny looked at her for an explanation and she said with a smile:

4

"They are neither upstairs nor downstairs, so to speak, but in a No-Man's-Land somewhere in between, which I imagine is a very uncomfortable position."

Then because the idea of Governesses rather caught her fancy, she decided she would write a novel about them.

The heroine would be very poor and very pretty, she told herself. She would get a post in a Ducal household, and of course, as the Duke was a widower, she would eventually marry him and live happily ever afterwards.

It seemed to Lara the type of novel she would like to read herself, and she was certain when it was completed she would find a publisher for it and make her fortune.

"Perhaps like Lord Byron I shall become famous overnight!"

There were also the Brontës, who she thought resembled herself, being Parson's daughters living in the wilds of Yorkshire. While one could hardly call Little Fladbury wild, it was certainly dull, and nothing happened from one year's end to the next.

In novels, she thought, there was always a grand house where the Squire lived.

He would either be young and handsome with his eye on a pretty village maiden, or else, if he were old and cantankerous, he would have a son who was dashing enough to wish to run away with the girl he loved.

Because Lara was an only child and had lived so much on her own, her head was full of stories. Only her mother had understood that the people who lived in her imagination were just as real, if not more so, than those she encountered every day.

Now as she rose from the table she thought with

satisfaction that she had written two chapters of her book in her neat hand-writing, but she was now undoubtedly stuck in the third.

It was where the heroine, having been recommended for a position in the Ducal household by a kind old lady who lived in the neighbourhood, was setting out for the ancestral Castle.

"How can I describe such a place without having seen one?" she asked.

She wondered whether it would be possible to ride over and look at the outside of one of the country houses that were not too far from Little Fladbury. But in the part of Essex where she lived there were no important mansions.

Ten or fifteen miles away there were, Lara knew, several houses of aristocrats, and she felt if she could see them it would be helpful.

But the only horse she and her father had to ride was growing old, and she doubted if Rollo would carry her ten miles, and certainly not twenty.

She knew that one of the farmers would lend her a cart-horse in an emergency, either to ride or attach to the gig, but again it was a question of distance.

She reckoned it would take far too long to travel at least ten miles each way and get back the same evening, and she could hardly spend the night under a hedge.

'I suppose all writers have the same difficulties that I am having,' she thought.

But that was poor consolation, and she looked at her manuscript a little ruefully before she thought she had better do as Nanny insisted and go outside in the garden.

Nanny was always interrupting and trying to prevent Lara from concentrating on her novel.

She knew in a way it was a kind of jealousy, for Nanny had for many years disliked the thought of her growing up and being able to think for herself.

And yet it was difficult to know what they would have done without Nanny to cook, clean the house, and look after her father as she had looked after Lady Hurlington until she died.

'I will walk down to the orchard,' Lara decided, 'and perhaps, besides pleasing Nanny, it will give me an idea of what I can say next.'

She went from the Study into the Hall where she saw that Nanny had placed on a chair the old sun-bonnet she wore in the garden, but her scarf which she wore over her shoulders when it was cold had obviously been taken upstairs.

Lara picked up her bonnet and was just going to leave the Vicarage by the garden door when there was a rat-tat from the front of the house.

She wondered who it could be.

It was too late for the postman, who had already been, and all the local people knew that her father was away conducting a Funeral in the next village to stand in for their incumbent who was on holiday.

Realising, when she did not come from the kitchen, that Nanny could not have heard the knock on the front door, Lara went to open it.

For a moment she stared at the visitor standing outside, then gave a cry of delight.

"Jane!" she exclaimed. "Jane! How exciting to see you!"

"It is lovely to see you, Lara," the woman replied.

"Come in!" Lara invited. "I am longing to hear all your news."

Jane Cooper, who was a young woman of twenty-four, stepped into the hall and looked at Lara a little

7

nervously as if she could hardly believe she was really pleased to see her.

Mr. Cooper, Jane's father, had been a retired School Master who had taught Lara for years until he died.

Jane had been born when her father was quite old. Her birth had killed her mother and that had been a great grief to Mr. Cooper, but he was compensated by the fact that he adored his only child.

He spent his time teaching her as he taught so many boys at the Public School where he had been for the main years of his teaching life.

When Lara's mother had realised how fortunate they were to have such an intelligent man living in Little Fladbury, she had asked him to take her daughter as a pupil, and although Jane was much older than she was, she and Lara had become friends.

But the two girls were very different characters.

Jane, perhaps because she had never had a mother's love, was shy, self-effacing, and very unsure of herself.

She grew, however, to be pretty in a rather nondescript manner, with fair hair and a clear pink-and-white complexion.

In her small face her main beauty was two sky-blue eyes that looked at the world either with surprise or with a shrinking reluctance to be involved in anything that was not straight-forward and simple.

In fact, despite her superior education, Lara often felt that Jane was younger than she was and even more unsophisticated.

It was disastrous when Mr. Cooper died, because his small pension died with him and this meant that Jane had to earn her own living.

The only possible position for which she was qualified was that of a Governess, and it was Lady Hurlington who found Jane employment with one of her husband's relatives who lived in a very different world from the one they occupied.

Jane had been extremely grateful and had gone to Lady Ludlow's house in London where she had three small children to teach and had been, Lara always understood, a success.

As she opened the door of the Study and Jane followed her in, Lara thought it was providential that she should have arrived 'at this particular moment when she was badly in need of information for the background to the book she was writing about the life of a Governess.

"Sit down, Jane," she said. "I suppose you have had luncheon, and it is too early for tea, but I will tell Nanny you are here and would like a cup of coffee."

"No, I want nothing, Lara, except your help," Jane replied.

"My help?" Lara repeated and smiled. "That is what I want from you!"

She thought Jane looked puzzled and she said quickly:

"Never mind that for the moment. Tell me what it is you want first, and I will talk afterwards."

Jane was taking off her white cotton gloves and when she had put them down she clasped her hands together and said:

"Oh, Lara . . . I am in such . . . trouble!"

The way she spoke told Lara it was serious and she asked:

"In trouble, Jane? How? What has happened?"

"I really do not know . . . how to . . . begin," Jane replied, "but the reason I came here today was to ask . . . your father if he would be kind . . . enough to give me another . . . reference."

"What happened to the one you had before?" Lara enquired.

"Your relation Lady Ludlow gave it to the Marquis of Keyston, where I am now employed."

"You have left Lady Ludlow?" Lara exclaimed. "I had no idea of that."

"It was not for anything I had done wrong," Jane said quickly, "but the two boys went to a Preparatory School and it was decided that the little girl should have lessons with some other children of her own age."

"Oh, poor Jane! So they did not want you any longer."

"I was very sorry to leave them," Jane went on. "I had been happy there and Lady Ludlow was very kind."

"So she found you a new position?"

Jane nodded.

"And what is wrong with that?"

She thought for a moment that Jane was not going to answer, and there was an expression in her blue eyes that Lara did not understand.

Then she said:

"Oh, Lara . . . it is so . . . frightening! I do not . . . know what to . . . do."

"Tell me everything from the very beginning," Lara suggested.

It flashed through her mind that Jane's revelations of what was happening in her position as Governess were exactly what she needed for her novel.

Then she told herself that was a very selfish thought, and she must concentrate on helping Jane,

10

who, she was quite certain, would never be able to help herself.

"When Lady Ludlow told me I was to go to the Marquis of Keyston I was rather frightened," Jane began, "because he is so . . . important."

"Who is he?" Lara asked. "I have never heard of him."

"He is a friend of the Prince of Wales and owns a great number of race horses. Lady Ludlow spoke of him in a way which told me she admired him very much."

"He sounds fascinating!" Lara said. "Go on, Jane. What is the Marquis's wife like?"

"He is not married," Jane answered. "I teach his niece, the only child of his elder brother, who died without having a son."

"Oh, I see that is why the present Marquis inherited."

"Yes, that is right," Jane agreed, "and Georgina is a nice little girl."

"How old is she?" Lara interposed.

"She is ten, but rather stupid and I am not able to teach her very much."

"And where does the Marquis live?"

"In an enormous house called 'Keyston Priory,'" Jane answered. "It has beautiful grounds, and I would be happy there, except . . ."

She stopped and bit on her lower lip as if it were trembling.

Lara's eyes were alight with interest.

"What has happened, Jane?" she asked. "Is it the Marquis who is making life difficult for you?"

She did not know quite how to phrase it, but she was sure in her imagination that a wicked villain, as in a Play, was menacing the gentle and pure maiden who was Jane, and only the hero could save her.

"No, it is . . . not the Marquis who is the . . . difficulty," Jane faltered, "but . . . his friend."

"What friend?"

"He is called Lord Magor . . . and he is quite . . . old."

Lara waited and Jane said, the words seeming to burst from her lips:

"Oh, Lara, I am frightened of him . . . and I do not know what to . . . do. I have to . . . leave . . . and there is . . . nowhere I can . . . go."

Lara drew her chair a little nearer to Jane's.

"What is he doing to frighten you?" she asked.

"He keeps coming into the School-Room in the evenings when I am . . . alone, and the night before last he tried to kiss me—Oh, Lara, I know it is wrong and wicked, but he will not listen when I . . . tell him to go . . . away."

"But you got away today?"

"I was just fortunate," Jane replied. "Georgina had a terrible toothache yesterday morning. In fact it was so bad that I told His Lordship's secretary, Mr. Simpson, who runs the house, that she would have to visit the Dentist."

"So you took her to London."

"That is right," Jane agreed, "and she saw the Dentist, who found she had an abscess in one of her teeth. She was so unwell that he insisted on her staying in bed today."

She paused for breath and went on:

"Her old Nanny came to London with us, and is staying with her in Keyston House there, which gave me a chance to catch a train which brought me here to you, but I must be careful not to miss the one that goes back at five o'clock."

"You will have to walk to the station, unless Papa returns with the trap," Lara said.

"I will leave in plenty of time," Jane replied.

"Go on about Lord Magor."

"He is always . . . staying at the Priory because the Marquis likes having him there. He has big parties, so I cannot see why Lord Magor should want to come and talk to me when the ladies who the Marquis invites are so beautiful and have the most glorious gowns you have ever seen."

"I want to know everything about them, too," Lara said. "But go on about Lord Magor. Surely you can tell him to leave you alone."

"He will not listen," Jane said. "He keeps telling me how pretty I am, and he is very . . . overpowering. Besides, it is . . . difficult to be rude to a gentleman who must be at least . . . forty."

'He is exactly the sort of man I would expect him to be,' Lara's imagination told her.

She was sure that Lord Magor was rather large and stout with a ruddy complexion, and smoked a huge cigar.

"I suppose," she asked, "you could not tell the Marquis about his friend and ask him to order Lord Magor to leave you alone?"

"Tell the . . . Marquis?" Jane repeated in horror. "I could not! As it is, I find it . . . difficult to say even good-morning or good-evening to him. He is . . . terrifying!"

"Why? In what way?" Lara asked.

"It is hard to . . . explain," Jane answered. "He is very cynical and autocratic, and appears to be contemptuous of everything and . . . everybody—and especially of me!"

"Oh, poor Jane!" Lara said sympathetically. "You seem to have got yourself into exactly the wrong sort of place."

She was going to add: 'For somebody like you,' then thought it would sound rather rude.

But she knew better than anybody how helpless Jane was in coping with even the small difficulties of life, let alone gentlemen who pursued her, obviously with evil intentions.

Lara was very innocent and was not certain exactly what that meant.

She only knew that the villains in the novels she had read and the stories which filled her mind were always pursuing innocent young maidens, not because they wished to marry them, but to offer them what was described as 'a fate worse than death.'

What that was she had no idea, but she knew it was something to do with the Ten Commandments.

Her father occasionally preached against 'sinners who deserved the fires of hell,' and the sinners unquestionably were the villains in her stories.

Now out of the blue Jane was giving her half-a-dozen new plots!

She felt her fingers itching to set them down in the neat books she had once used for her lessons, but which now contained two chapters of her precious novel.

"Tell me about the Marquis," she said, and thought Jane shuddered before she said:

"He is . . . terrifying, and I never go near him if I can . . . help it. But Lord Magor is much, much worse. Oh, Lara, what can I do to . . . make him . . . leave me . . . alone?"

14

Before Lara could answer she said:

"It is no use—I simply cannot stay at the Priory, and that is why I came to ask your father if he would be kind enough to give me a reference. If I ask Mr. Simpson for mine, he may guess that I am trying to find ... another situation."

"How will you get one without his knowing you are leaving?" Lara asked.

"I thought ..." Jane said hesitatingly, "... that I would ... write to a ... Domestic Bureau where I know the servants come from, and then later ask ... Lady Ludlow if she will ... recommend me."

"I am sure she will do that."

"Yes, but I do not wish her to tell the Marquis what I am doing until I actually have ... somewhere else to ... go. You know I have no home, and since Papa's relations live in the North of England I cannot afford to go and stay with them."

"You can always come here," Lara said.

Jane's eyes lit up.

"Do you really mean that?"

"Of course I mean it. I would love to have you and so would Papa. He will write you a glowing reference or, if you like, I can write you out the same one that Mama gave you and sign it with her name."

"Do you ... think that would be quite ... honest?" Jane asked.

"Of course it would! It would only be like Mama giving you the same reference twice, if she had thought about it at the time."

"Yes, I suppose so," Jane said doubtfully, "and it is very ... very kind of you, Lara, but I still have to go back and ... face Lord Magor until I have found ... somewhere else."

"What is he like?" Lara asked.

15

"I suppose he was rather good looking when he was young. The Housekeeper, Mrs. Brigstow, was talking about him one day and said he had a reputation with women! I suppose that is why he cannot . . . understand why I do not want him to . . . kiss me."

Lara gave an exclamation and said:

"You know, this is exactly what I was certain happened to Governesses in the big houses where gentlemen think, because the women are neither upstairs nor downstairs but in the middle, they are 'fair game.'"

She was puzzling it out for herself when she saw that Jane was looking shocked.

"That sounds . . . horrid, Lara!" she cried. "But I suppose it is . . . true."

"I was saying to Nanny just before you came," Lara went on, "that Mama said once that a Governess's life was somewhere between Heaven and Hell, in a No-Man's-Land of their own, and that is where you are, Jane."

"I know," Jane said with a little sigh, "but it . . . frightens me, and when I . . . lock myself in my room at night, I am always . . . afraid that somehow . . . Lord Magor may . . . get in."

"How could he do that?"

"He could not . . . and it is . . . silly of me even to think of it . . . but I cannot sleep and in the morning I have a . . . headache, and feel so . . . ill that I can hardly teach Georgina. I know really I just . . . want to . . . run away and never . . . never go . . . back."

The way Jane spoke told Lara that she was indeed very upset.

In fact, she knew now she looked at her that her

face was unnaturally pale and she had dark shadows under her eyes.

Lara remembered that Jane had always been very highly strung.

If she had ever had a disagreement with her father or anybody else she would cry herself sick and would lie on her bed sobbing and refusing to have anything to eat.

It flashed through her mind that if Jane had a nervous breakdown she would be dismissed and might find it impossible to get another job.

"What you really need, Jane, is a holiday," she said. "Have you made any arrangement as to when you should have one?"

"I forgot to ask about it when I was engaged," Jane replied. "Anyway, I do not want a holiday—I have nowhere to go."

"I really think you ought to have one," Lara insisted.

"How can I?" Jane asked. "And I suppose things will be better when the Marquis goes away and does not have so many parties. I understand from the servants that when the Season starts in London he only occasionally comes down to the Priory from Saturday to Monday."

"But you think Lord Magor will be staying with him?"

"He always seems to be there," Jane answered. "There has only been one party he did not attend ever since I have been at the Priory."

"I do see it is a problem," Lara said, "but you must stand up to him. You must tell him that if he does not leave you alone, you will go to the Marquis."

"I would be much too afraid to do that," Jane answered, "and therefore I would not sound . . . convincing and he would not . . . believe me."

There were tears in her eyes as she continued:

"It is no use, Lara—I cannot stay there any longer. I must . . . find . . . somewhere else to go. Do you think I . . . dare write to . . . Lady Ludlow?"

"Although she is Papa's relation, I have never met her," Lara said. "Is she the sort of person who will understand?"

"I honestly do not know," Jane replied. "She was kind to me when I was living in her house and teaching her children, but she was not often there."

"What do you mean?" Lara asked.

"She moves in the same society as the Marquis, and therefore is always with the Prince and Princess of Wales and smart people like that."

"It sounds fascinating," Lara said. "Go on!"

"Of course the only big parties I saw were the ones Lady Ludlow gave herself, and that was four or five times a year. There were two Hunt Balls, several shoots, and the garden-parties she gave in the summer."

"I wish I could have seen the parties too!"

Jane gave a wistful little smile.

"I am afraid I used to peep through the bannisters with the servants to see the ladies going down to dinner! They were covered in jewels and wearing gowns that were so low in front that I am sure your Papa would have thought them very shocking!"

Lara smiled, but she did not answer.

Her father had often described to her how beautiful her mother had looked at the Balls to which he had been asked as a young man.

"But surely you talked to Lady Ludlow when she was not having parties?" Lara asked.

"I used to take the children down to the Drawing-Room at five o'clock," Jane replied. "They hated going downstairs and used to whine and complain all the time I was dressing them in their best clothes."

"Then what did you do?" Lara persisted.

"I would go into the Drawing-Room, stand inside the doorway, and wait until Lady Ludlow said:

"'Oh, here are the children! Come and kiss me, darlings.'

"As they went towards her she would ask:

"'Have they been good today, Miss Cooper?'

"'Yes, M' Lady,' I would reply.

"Then as she kissed them I would curtsy and go upstairs again."

"Is that all?" Lara asked.

"Yes, until I fetched them."

"What happened then?"

"When I went into the Drawing-Room, Lady Ludlow would look up and say:

"'Here is Miss Cooper. Now run along to bed, my darlings, and do not forget to say your prayers.'

"Sometimes she would look at me and say:

"'You will be sure they remember their prayers, Miss Cooper?'

"'Yes, M' Lady,' I would say. Then as the children reached me I would curtsy again and take them upstairs."

Lara laughed.

"You make her sound completely unapproachable. But Jane, this is exactly what I want to hear, and now you must let me tell you my news. I am writing a book!"

"A book?" Jane questioned.

"A novel," Lara explained, "and the heroine is a poor Governess, just like you, who marries the Duke

19

in the end. So perhaps you will marry the Marquis and make my story come true!"

Jane looked at her in horror.

"I would certainly not marry His Lordship even if he asked me!" she cried. "He frightens me so much that when he says 'Good-morning, Miss Cooper!' I find it almost...impossible to...answer him."

"Then perhaps you will marry Lord Magor," Lara said without thinking.

Jane gave a little cry before she answered:

"That is unkind, Lara—really unkind. I hate him—I hate him! I know I shall...never be able to...escape from him and in the end he will get what...he wants."

"I am sorry," Lara said quickly. "I did not mean to upset you! But Jane, what does he want?"

"Something that is wrong and wicked! But I am good, I have always been good, and Papa would not expect me to be anything else," Jane replied passionately.

"No, of course not," Lara agreed.

She saw the tears come into Jane's eyes, and now she put her arms around her and said:

"I am only teasing you as I used to do when I was little, and you used to get angry with me. Forgive me, Jane dear, and I will help you somehow, I promise I will!"

"Nobody can help me," she said miserably. "There is nothing anybody can do, and when I go back to the Priory tomorrow I am sure...Lord Magor will be...there...waiting for me."

"Then you must not go back."

Lara suddenly knew as she spoke it was the only answer.

She could feel Jane trembling against her, and the

hand that was holding the handkerchief to her eyes was shaking.

"Now listen, Jane," she said, "you have to be sensible about this. You must stay here and write to Lady Ludlow to ask for her help, and also to the Domestic Bureau in London."

"I . . . I could not . . . leave without . . . giving in my . . . notice," Jane said in a trembling voice. "If I just . . . walked out like that . . . nobody would give me a job."

"Are you sure?"

"Absolutely sure!" Jane said. "Mr. Simpson, who engages the staff at the Priory, is always saying that he would never give a reference to anybody who leaves without giving proper notice! When one of the house-maids ran away to get married, he said, and I heard him:

" 'That puts a finish to any employment as far as she is concerned! It is a disgraceful way to behave, and sets a bad example to everybody else in the house!' "

"How long does a notice have to be?" Lara asked.

"At least a month," Jane answered, "and sometimes longer, if they cannot find . . . somebody to fill the . . . place."

Her handkerchief went up to her eyes again as she said:

"How can I bear another . . . month of . . . waiting and listening at night for . . . Lord Magor to come to the School-Room? I think I shall go mad!"

She sounded so distraught that Lara could only hold her a little closer.

"Listen, Jane," she said, "I am going to tell Nanny you are here and ask her to make you a cup of tea. You will feel better after you have had a rest."

21

"I cannot rest until I can leave the Priory and never, never see Lord Magor again!"

Jane drew in her breath. Then she suddenly said:

"Supposing . . . just supposing that at the next . . . place I go to the parents are friends of his and he . . . follows me?"

"He certainly sounds despicable," Lara said. "What he needs is a good sharp lesson, which I suppose only another man could give him!"

She thought for a moment.

Then once again a plot was weaving itself in her mind and, just as she did when she was alone, she could see things happening as if they were pictures moving in front of her eyes.

She could imagine Jane trembling in the School-Room, she could hear the heavy footsteps coming up the stairs, she could see Lord Magor entering to menace her, his eyes flashing fire, his hands reaching out towards poor Jane, who was shrinking away from him in sheer, unbridled terror!

Then suddenly Lord Magor would be stopped and unable to proceed any further.

He had met his match! He would be confounded and vanquished as the villain always was in any story where good triumphs over evil.

She gave a sudden cry.

"Jane! I know exactly what we must do!"

"What is that?" Jane asked dully.

"You must not go back to the Priory," Lara said. "You must stay here, rest, have a holiday, and Nanny will look after you."

"You know I have to go back," Jane answered. "I have to go back and 'work out my notice,' as the servants say. If I walk out, I will never get a good position again, not even with a reference from your father."

"Yes, you will," Lara said. "I am planning it all out in my mind."

She took her arms from around Jane and sat with her fingers holding her small pointed chin as if to help her to think.

Jane wiped her eyes and looked at her apprehensively.

"It is no use, Lara," she said. "You are very kind, and I know you are trying to help me, but I am . . . caught in a trap . . . and there is . . . no way . . . out."

Her voice broke on the last words and Lara rose to her feet as if it were easier to talk standing up.

"Now listen, Jane," she said. "I am sure that before you left the Priory to come to London you looked ill, and perhaps you even complained to Nanny, or whoever else was with the child, that you were upset."

"I do not remember saying anything," Jane replied. "but they must have realised I was not myself because Nanny, who is usually rather disagreeable, said:

"'That's all right, Miss Cooper. You go and see your friends and don't worry about Georgina. She'll be happy enough with me.'"

"Well, there you are!" Lara said with satisfaction.

"As a matter of fact," Jane went on, as if Lara had not spoken, "Nanny prefers having Georgina to herself. She is jealous of me and thinks Governesses are unnecessary and, in her words, 'trouble-makers.'"

Lara laughed.

"I am sure that is the last thing you are, Jane!"

"I try not to be, and I certainly do not want any . . . trouble for . . . anyone else. I am in . . . enough . . . myself!"

"Well, this is what you are going to do to get out of it," Lara said.

Jane looked at her, but her blue eyes were dull, her lips quivering, and her face very pale.

It struck Lara that she was, in fact, frightened to the point where she might easily collapse and be really ill, which, in regard to her future, would be disastrous.

She sat down again beside Jane and said:

"Now do not speak until I have finished telling you my plan. You will stay here, Nanny will look after you, and you will eat and sleep until you feel really well again."

Jane opened her lips to protest, but Lara put up her hand to command silence.

"I will catch the five o'clock train back to London," she said, "and tell Georgina's Nanny that when you were here you became ill and I have come to take your place."

Jane started.

"But that is ridiculous! Of course you cannot do that."

"Why not?" Lara asked. "You know as well as I do that having been taught by your father I am just as capable of teaching Georgina as you are."

"Nobody could teach her," Jane said. "She is a very stupid child, and you are not the sort of person to be a Governess, Lara. You are a real Lady, like your mother."

Lara laughed.

"Being a 'real Lady' does not make us any money, and certainly does not entitle me to go to Balls glittering with jewels or to be upstairs with the Marquis and Lord Magor."

She felt the little shudder that went through Jane at Lord Magor's name and went on:

"I think I can deal with him much more effectively than you can. In fact, I intend to teach him a lesson which he will never forget."

"Oh, Lara, you are not to go near him! You will not speak to him!" Jane said. "I could not allow you to do so."

"You are not going to be able to stop me," Lara said, "and, Jane, unlike you I am not afraid of him."

Jane gave a sigh that was almost a sob.

"I suppose that is because you are who you are, but I cannot...help being...frightened. Even to think of him makes me feel...almost sick with...fear."

"I know," Lara said soothingly, "and that is why you could not possibly stand another month of it, so I am going to work out your notice for you."

"No, no!" Jane exclaimed.

Lara went on:

"What I am going to tell first Georgina and her Nanny, and then the Marquis himself, is that when you visited me in the country you developed a rash which the Doctor thinks might be measles or chicken-pox. Therefore you could not possibly take the risk of passing the infection on to Georgina."

Jane looked at her wide-eyed, but she did not say anything and Lara continued:

"As I am a friend of yours and I was, as it happens, at this very moment looking for a position as a Governess, I agreed out of kindness, and so as to cause no inconvenience to the Marquis, to take your place and teach Georgina until you are well enough to return to your post."

Her voice was triumphant as she finished:

"As they will suffer no inconvenience by the exchange, I cannot believe that anyone, least of all the Marquis, will refuse to employ me."

25

"Do you really . . . think he will . . . believe you?" Jane asked.

"Of course he will," Lara said. "Why should he question that you, in staying away, were only thinking of what was best for the child?"

"I cannot let . . . you do . . . it," Jane exclaimed.

But Lara knew by the tone of her voice that she was weakening.

"It is what I am going to do," she said, "and neither Nanny nor you is going to stop me."

She knew as she spoke that Nanny might be the stumbling-block, and she said quickly:

"I am going to the kitchen to talk to Nanny now. Make yourself comfortable, Jane dear, and do not worry about anything. I promise you, I will cope with the Marquis, Lord Magor, 'Uncle Tom Cobleigh,' and all!"

She laughed as she spoke.

Then without listening to Jane's cry of protest she went from the Study, closing the door behind her.

chapter two

DRIVING towards Keyston House in Park Lane, Lara
admitted to herself that she felt rather nervous.

At the same time she kept thinking what an adventure it was and how good her book would be once
she had the facts that would be completely authentic
not only about the social life in a large house, but also
about a real-life villain.

She knew it was only because she was frightened
of Lord Magor that reluctantly, still protesting to the
very last minute, Jane had allowed her to take her
place.

"They will not want you to look after the child if
you have measles," Lara argued, "and if they refuse
and say she can manage without a Governess, then
I will just come back. What have we got to lose, one
way or another?"

This was indisputable, and gradually she wore

27

down Jane into agreeing that it was at least worth her having a few days rest, even if she could not take any longer.

Nanny was far more difficult to convince.

"I never heard such a thing!" she exclaimed. "You going off on your own to stay in a strange house!"

"I am not going as a visitor," Lara argued, "and I shall be just as safe and unimportant as Jane has been."

Before telling Nanny what she intended to do, she had made Jane promise on her word of honour that she would not mention Lord Magor's name.

"You know what Nanny is like," she said, "and she would have a fit if she knew you had been approached by him, let alone me!"

"Yes, I know that," Jane said miserably, "and that is why, Lara, I should not let you go. After all, I am older than you and should be able to take care of myself."

This was one thing Lara knew Jane was incapable of doing, and she was determined, because she felt Lord Magor was behaving so abominably, to frighten him as he had frightened Jane.

She had seen in her imagination exactly what she would do, and while Nanny went on protesting volubly every time Lara appeared or was doing her packing, she went into her father's bedroom and opened the bottom drawer of his wardrobe.

In it were various things which had belonged to his father and which he had taken from the family house before it was sold.

There were some miniatures of Hurley grandparents, sketches done by her mother when she was a girl, and what Lara was seeking, a pair of duelling pistols.

When her father had first brought them back to the Vicarage he had shown them to her proudly and said that he treasured them because they had first been used by his grandfather in a duel during the reign of George IV.

"I am afraid the duel was over a very attractive lady whom my grandfather and another Peer were both courting," Lara's father had said.

"Who won?" Lara had asked.

"I am glad to say that my grandfather did, and he fought another duel with the same pistols in which he was also the victor."

"How exciting!" Lara had exclaimed. "He must have been very dashing to be involved in two duels!"

Her father's story had naturally made Lara's imagination begin to invent stories about her great-grandfather, and she had persuaded him to let her fire the pistols her ancestor had used so effectively.

Because she had no wish to kill anything that lived, she drew a target on a piece of cardboard, pinned it onto one of the trees in the garden, and her father showed her how to aim at it.

When she hit several bull's-eyes in quick succession he told her she could now consider herself quite a good shot.

"Not that you are likely, my dearest, to be fighting any duels," he said, "but it is not a bad idea for a woman to know how to defend herself."

"Against whom, Papa?" Lara had enquired.

There was a little hesitation before her father replied:

"I suppose the right answer is thieves and robbers."

Lara had known perceptively that what he was going to say was gentlemen who approached her when she was unwilling to accept their advances.

"Even if Jane had owned a pistol, she would have been too afraid to frighten Lord Magor with it," she told herself.

She was quite certain that not only would Jane be unable to fire a pistol, but that she, being able to hit a bull's-eye, could certainly hit a man.

The feeling that the pistols were in her luggage, slipped in amongst her clothes when Nanny was not looking, was reassuring.

Although of course she told herself there was always the chance that while he admired Jane, Lord Magor might not admire her.

At the same time, she would have been very stupid if she had not realised when she looked at her reflection in the mirror before she left, that she was very pretty.

The Hurleys had perhaps inherited their looks from her dashing ancestor, the first Lord Hurlington, so that the ladies of the family were beauties, the gentlemen extremely handsome.

Most of the women who came to the Church in Little Fladbury, Lara often thought, went to admire her father because he looked irresistibly handsome in his surplice.

They certainly sat rapt and attentive while he preached rather long and dull sermons from the pulpit.

No one could have said that her mother also had not been lovely, and it was from her that Lara had inherited her hair that was more red than gold, and seemed in the sunshine or candlelight to halo her face with a fiery glow.

"If I had green eyes," she told herself, "I would look like a Siren or even the villainess in a novel."

The latter were always described as having red hair, green eyes, and a body which moved like a serpent's.

Instead her eyes were grey flecked with gold, and because she was staring at her reflection intently, she looked very young and a little frightened of what she was about to do.

"I must remember," she warned herself, "that I am supposed to be at least twenty-three or twenty-four years of age because otherwise I shall be considered much too young to teach anybody."

She had written herself out a reference just in case anybody asked for it, and signed it with her father's name.

Jane, trying to be as helpful as she could, thought it was unlikely, as she was only supposed to be teaching Georgina on a temporary basis, that they would ask for many details about her life.

"But I feel very...nervous," she added, "that if they make too many enquiries about you they will find out...who you are."

"You know as well as I do that no one has ever heard of this benighted, out-of-the-way place," Lara answered, "nor is the Social World aware of Papa, let alone me."

Jane knew that was true and she said:

"Please, Lara, do be careful! Supposing...just supposing Lord Magor...hurts you? I should never ...forgive...myself."

"Hurts me? How could he hurt me? You say he tried to kiss you, and I admit that sounds horrible, but he is hardly likely to knock me down or beat me."

Jane did not answer and Lara had the feeling that she was turning something over in mind.

Then she said, as if she were trying to convince herself:

"I am sure it will be all right, and if he does frighten you, you must just run away and come home."

"I promise you that is what I will do," Lara answered, "but for Heaven's sake, do not say anything like that to Papa or Nanny or they will arrive the next day at the Priory to take me away."

"I will be very, very careful," Jane promised, "but I should stop you from doing this . . . although I know you are only . . . trying to . . . help me."

"I am being very selfish, as it happens," Lara said, "because it will give me the background I need for my novel. Oh, Jane, if it is a success, then you can share the proceeds with me, because it will all be due to you that it is authentic."

She had packed her manuscripts in her trunk.

'I should have time to write in the evenings,' she thought, 'when the child has gone to bed, and I will also take notes of everything that happens.'

She wanted to hear a great deal more about the parties at Keyston Priory from Jane, but she knew it was more important to learn what her duties were supposed to be, and what lessons she had been teaching Georgina.

"The child is really very stupid," Jane said, "although I cannot think why she should be when the Keyston family have the reputation of being clever Statesmen and have also distinguished themselves as soldiers."

"Is there a history of the family?" Lara asked.

"I expect there is in the Library," Jane answered, "but I never have time to read. By the time I have put Georgina to bed and tidied the School-Room I am too terrified that Lord Magor will come to see me to be able to . . . concentrate on . . . reading a book."

Lara could not help feeling that Jane was making things worse than they need be.

"After all, he is only a man," she told herself, "and what could Jane mean by saying he might hurt her?"

It puzzled her a little, but she had so many other

things to think about that she had forgotten about Lord Magor by the time the hackney carriage reached Keyston House.

As the horse stopped she knew this was the test as to whether she could stay, or would be sent away.

She had remembered to ask Jane what was the name of Georgina's Nanny, knowing how her own Nurse disliked strangers addressing her familiarly as 'Nanny.'

"Nesbit, Miss Nesbit," Jane said.

"Should I ask for her when I arrive, or will there be a secretary like the one at the Priory whom I should see first?"

"Mr. Simpson is at the Priory at the moment because the Marquis is there," Jane replied. "When he returns to London, Mr. Simpson goes ahead of him to have everything prepared and ready for his arrival."

"Then the best thing I can do is to ask for the Nanny," Lara decided, "and explain to her what has happened."

"I . . . I hope that is right . . . I think so . . . oh, dear . . . I wish you were not doing this!" Jane stammered.

"We cannot go all over that again," Lara answered, "and now I think I hear Jacobs outside with the wheelbarrow, and I had better leave."

There was no other way she could get her trunk to the station except by ordering Jacobs to push it there in the wheel-barrow.

Her father had taken Rollo in the trap to go to the neighbouring village.

Although Lara might have asked one of the farmers for the loan of a wagon, she thought it would be a mistake for anybody except Nanny and Jane to know what she was doing.

As the Vicarage and the Church were at the far end

33

of the village, nobody saw her set off a few minutes later to walk briskly down the twisting lane which eventually reached the high road which led to the station for Little Fladbury and other villages.

It was actually only a Halt and as there was no permanent employee in charge of it, anyone wishing to travel to London or on the down line to other parts of Essex had to manipulate the signal himself.

Although Lara's trunk did not contain very much it was made of heavy leather and Jacobs pushed the wheel-barrow onto the platform with a grunt of relief, pulling a dirty handkerchief from the pocket of his corduroy trousers to mop his forehead as he did so.

"That be a long step, Miss Lara," he said.

"I am very grateful to you, Jacobs," Lara replied, "and will you please work the signal for me?"

Jacobs did as he was asked. Lara had had so much to ask Jane that she had not left home until the last minute. So she had only a very short wait before she could see the smoke from the engine in the distance.

A few seconds later the train drew noisily in to stop beside the platform.

The guard got out to supervise her trunk being lifted into the Van, then found her a seat in the carriage labelled *'Ladies Only,'* while the second man driving the engine reset the signal.

Then they were off and Lara leaned out of the window to wave good-bye to Jacobs who was, however, already wheeling his barrow off the platform.

"This is a real adventure!" Lara told herself.

She was saying the same thing as the hackney carriage stopped at Keyston House.

It looked very impressive with its porticoed front door standing back from Park Lane with a high wall enclosing what Lara guessed was a garden filled with trees at the back of it.

'It must be lovely to be so rich that you can afford to keep up a huge house in the country and another in London,' she thought.

The Cabby obligingly stepped down to ring the bell, and almost immediately it was opened by a footman in a very smart livery of dark blue and yellow with large silver buttons bearing the Marquis's crest.

By this time the Cabby had lifted her trunk from the front of the carriage and Lara saw the footman staring in surprise at the arrival of what was obviously an unexpected visitor.

She walked up the two marble steps to the front door.

"I wish to see Miss Nesbit," she said, "who I understand is with Lady Georgina, and please allow my trunk to wait in the Hall until I have spoken to her."

Although she did not realise it Lara spoke in quite a composed and authoritative manner and the footman immediately replied respectfully:

"I'll tell Miss Nesbit you're here, Ma'am."

"Thank you."

The flunkey led the way across the Hall and opened the door and Lara was shown into what she thought must be a Morning-Room.

It was attractively furnished with pictures which she knew at a glance were very valuable, and French furniture which she had studied in her books and had always longed actually to see.

While she waited she moved around the room looking at the pictures, reading the artist's names, and knowing that the price of just one of them would have kept her and her father in comfort, even luxury, for several years.

There had been pictures, perhaps not so good and certainly not so valuable, in the family house which had to be sold, and Lady Hurlington had often said to Lara:

"It is very silly to have regrets, but I often wish, dearest, that you had known what it was like to live in a big house, as I did when I was a girl, with lots of servants."

She had sighed before she added:

"I would love you to attend huge dinner-parties and of course dance in Ball-Rooms lit by crystal chandeliers to the sound of a dozen violins."

"It must have been very romantic, Mama."

"It was," her mother had replied, "but not so romantic as falling in love with your Papa, and living in a small rather shabby Vicarage, and being very, very happy."

There was no need to ask her mother if she had any regrets for giving up the life she had enjoyed as a girl.

But although she had never said so, Lara thought she must have enjoyed staying with her father-in-law at the family mansion where there were also a great many servants to see to the comfort of everybody who lived there.

"I wonder if I shall ever have a chance to see what Mama gave up when she married Papa and what we lost when Grandpapa was so extravagant," Lara thought.

The door opened and the footman returned.

"Nanny asks if you'll come upstairs, Ma'am," he said, "as she can't leave Her Ladyship."

Lara followed the footman up an impressive carved staircase to the first landing.

Then he went through a green baize door which led to another staircase not so impressive, and up to the second floor where there were a number of doors behind which Lara thought must be the main bedrooms of the house.

They walked down a long passage at the end of which he knocked on a door which was opened by a woman who Lara knew at once was 'Nanny.'

She was almost a carbon-copy of her own Nanny, in her grey dress with a starched white collar round her neck and a wide waistband clasped in front with a silver buckle.

She had starched cuffs caught with pearl buttons, and her grey hair was drawn back severely from the lined, kindly face.

She also had a firm mouth and chin which reflected years of giving orders which had to be obeyed.

Nanny stared at Lara with a look of surprise before she said in an uncompromising voice:

"You wished to see me?"

"I have brought a message from Miss Jane Cooper."

Nanny did not reply for a moment and as the footman walked away Lara said:

"I have something to explain to you. Could I come in?"

"You say you've come from Miss Cooper?" Nanny asked and she sounded suspicious.

"Yes," Lara answered.

A little reluctantly it seemed Nanny opened the door wider.

"Come in," she invited, "but do not talk too loud. Her Ladyship's asleep. She's been restless all day and it's the best thing that could happen. But I don't want her woken."

"Miss Cooper told me she had an abscess in a tooth."

"That's what the Dentist says it is," Nanny said, as if she were inclined to disagree with him.

Now she was inside the room, Lara saw it was a comfortable Sitting-Room and she had the idea, although she might have been wrong, that it was not the ordinary School-Room used by Georgina, but this was in fact a Boudoir of one of the guest-rooms.

"You'd better sit down," Nanny said.

Lara chose a sofa covered with a glossy flowered chintz and Nanny took a seat opposite her.

"Well?" she asked. "What's this all about?"

"I am afraid, Miss Nesbit, you will be rather upset when you hear what I have to tell you."

"What's happened?" Nanny asked.

"Miss Cooper came to see me in the country, where I have been living," Lara replied, "and she did not seem at all well. In fact, after luncheon I asked the doctor to have a look at her and he is almost certain that she has measles."

"Measles?" Nanny exclaimed, with what was almost a shriek.

Then before Lara could speak she said:

"That's all right. Her Ladyship's had it!"

"Oh, I am so glad," Lara said. "Miss Cooper was so frightened that she might have already infected the child."

"All the same there's a number of people at the Priory who've not had the measles," Nanny went on, "including two house-maids who wait on the School-Room."

"That was another thing which worried Miss Cooper," Lara said.

She was thinking as she spoke that she had been very quick in changing her story when she had learned the Lady Georgina had already had measles.

This was obviously something which Jane had not known, but it did not matter one way or the other as it would be impossible for her, anyway, to work for at least a fortnight or three weeks.

"Well, I'm very sorry to hear this," Nanny said after a moment. "I have always said that with those childhood ailments it's better to have them when you're young. You suffer more when you're older."

"That is what the doctor said," Lara answered, "and Miss Cooper felt that the only way she could make amends was to find somebody else to take her place temporarily."

She saw Nanny stiffen, but before she could speak Lara continued:

"I have just left my previous place because my pupil is too old to require a Governess any longer, and so as Miss Cooper was very anxious that you should not be inconvenienced in any way, I said that I would be glad to come and teach Lady Georgina until the doctor is sure Miss Cooper is no longer infectious."

Nanny looked doubtful.

"I don't know what to say," she answered. "It wouldn't really hurt Her Ladyship to have a holiday from her lessons."

Lara had expected this to happen and smiled.

"I am sure she would much rather be with you," she said, "but Miss Cooper was very anxious not to give you any extra to do when she told me how hard you work already. So, if I could just keep Lady Georgina amused for an hour or so a day it would, I am sure, make it easier for you than it would be otherwise."

She saw by the expression on Nanny's face that she was rather surprised at her attitude.

And after a moment she said almost grudgingly:

"Well, as you're here, and I presume you're a

friend of Miss Cooper's, you'd better stay for tonight at any rate."

"That is very kind of you," Lara said. "If you had not wanted me I do not know what I could do, as I doubt if there is a train to take me back to the country at this hour."

"I suppose Miss Cooper's been visiting you," Nanny said. "She did say she was going to see some friends."

"That is right," Lara said. "I was staying with Lord Hurlington, as it is his daughter I have been teaching, and Miss Cooper's father lived in the same village before he died."

She thought, although she was not sure, that Nanny was impressed when she mentioned the name of a Lord, before she asked:

"What is your name?"

"Wade . . . Lara Wade."

She had chosen the name because she thought it sounded rather prim and proper. There had been a spinster in Little Fladbury called Wade who had taught rather inadequately in the Sunday School.

"Well, Miss Wade, you'll understand that it's not up to me," Nanny said briskly, "to decide whether you stay with us until Miss Cooper's better. It's for His Lordship, or rather his secretary, Mr. Simpson, who engages the staff, to decide. You'll see him when we go back to the Priory tomorrow."

"I hope he will allow me to help you," Lara said, "and I am very much looking forward to seeing the Priory after all Miss Cooper has told me about it."

"I expect she admires it as everybody else does," Nanny said indifferently, almost as if she would not demean herself to be enthusiastic.

"I think," Lara said, "Miss Cooper feels she is very

lucky to be able to work in such an historic place with somebody as kind as you have been to her."

She was sure as she spoke that Nanny had been nothing of the sort, but merely jealous and obstructive.

But her mother had often said to her:

"You should always praise people for being the opposite of what they are and hope you will shame them into changing themselves."

Lara had laughed.

"You mean, Mama, that if you tell a miser he is generous and somebody who is cruel that he is gentle, they will change?"

"Exactly!" Lady Hurlington said. "Sometimes— just sometimes—I have known it to work!"

Lara had laughed and she knew now that Nanny was pleased at what she had said and had relaxed a little.

"As there's a little time before supper, Miss Wade," she said crisply, "I expect you'd like to take off your bonnet and cape and wash your hands."

She spoke almost as if Lara were a child who had to be reminded, and at the same time she gave the bell which hung from the ceiling a good tug.

As she did so Lara thought with a leap of her heart that she had won!

She had crossed the threshold, she had been accepted, and she could already visualise how much being here was going to improve the third chapter of her book.

* * *

When Lara met Georgina the next morning she was exactly as Jane had described her.

A pretty child but lethargic, she seemed to have little interest in anything that was going on around her.

Nanny took Lara into the bedroom, where Georgina was sitting up in bed eating her breakfast.

When she explained that Miss Cooper was ill and had sent a friend to take her place until she got better, it appeared to arouse little curiosity in Georgina, who continued to eat her egg.

Only as she finished the last mouthful did she say:

"I do not want to be given any lessons! I hate verbs!"

"So do I," Lara agreed. "It took me a long time to be able to remember them."

Georgina made no comment and Lara went on:

"Before we do any lessons, I hope you will show me your lovely home where we are going today. I am so looking forward to seeing it."

"It is very big," Georgina said, as if that were a disadvantage.

"I have been living in a very small house," Lara answered, "so I shall find a big one very exciting, but you must save me from getting lost."

There was just a flicker of interest in Georgina's eyes before she answered:

"No one gets lost at the Priory and the house-maids are afraid to walk about at night in case they see the ghost."

"Is there a ghost?" Lara asked. "How thrilling! Do tell me about it."

"Now that's enough of that talk," Nanny interposed sharply. "You know as well as I do that it frightens Nelly and Bessie and we'll have them screaming all over the place that they've seen the 'White Lady' or the 'Grey Monk' or some such nonsense."

"Have you ever seen a ghost?" Lara asked.

"If there's people creeping about the corridors at the Priory, they're not ghosts!" Nanny said sharply.

As if she thought she had said too much she walked

out of the bedroom leaving Lara alone with Georgina.

"Nelly's terrified of ghosts," she said in a low voice. "Once I dressed up in a sheet and said 'Boo!' to Nelly when she came into the room. She screamed and dropped a tray, and Nanny was very angry."

Lara laughed.

"I am not surprised. If people are frightened it makes them do all sorts of silly things."

"Perhaps you will be frightened when you get to the Priory," Georgina said.

"I hope not," Lara replied, "and I will not scream, even if I see a ghost."

"Lots of people are frightened of Uncle Ulric," Georgina said impulsively.

Lara guessed that this was the Marquis and she asked:

"Why?"

"Because he is a frightening person," Georgina replied.

Then as if she had no wish to answer any more questions she said:

"I want to get up. Tell Nanny I want to get up."

"Yes, of course."

Lara rose and opened the door to find Nanny was in the Sitting-Room collecting a number of things that were scattered about which would obviously have to be packed.

"Georgina wants to get up," she said, wondering if she was right to speak of the child without her title, "and do let me help you, Miss Nesbit."

Nanny appeared surprised that she should offer.

Then she held out a miscellaneous collection of things she had in her hands and said:

"They're for the trunk in the corner. I'll see to Her Ladyship."

Lara put all the things into the large trunk which

she noticed was made of a very expensive well-polished leather.

This was just another example of wealth, and she thought with a twist of her lips that the one person who would look like a beggar-maid at the Priory would be herself.

She had in fact been so ashamed of her old bonnet that she had asked Jane if she might borrow hers.

It was only a cheap straw, decorated with blue ribbons which matched Jane's eyes, but it was in good condition.

Putting it on her head, Lara thought it looked slightly theatrical with her red hair, but at the same time she could not have appeared in her old straw which was sadly out of date and, as she had already told Nanny, might fall to bits at any moment.

"Take anything else of mine you require," Jane said, "but I am afraid my clothes are not very smart."

"I expect I shall be green with envy when I see the gowns which are worn by the Marquis's guests."

"They are absolutely fantastic!" Jane answered. "They cost pounds and pounds to buy, and some of the beauties in London never wear them more than once."

"What happens to them after that?" Lara asked with interest.

"They become a perk for their Lady's-maids, who sell them."

"What an extraordinary idea!"

"Oh, no, it is quite usual amongst Ladies of Fashion," Jane replied. "I have often thought that if I had the money I would try to buy my clothes in that way. But as you know, Lara, I have to save every penny in case I am thrown out of work."

"Yes, of course," Lara agreed.

At the same time she hoped that Jane would have a few things she could borrow and which would not look as shabby as the gowns she had worn for years, some of which had become too tight because she had grown, and because they had been washed so frequently.

"As you will be using my room," Jane said, "you will find everything there waiting for you, and if you like I will give you the gown I have on."

As Lara thought it was rather ugly, she decided that she might as well wear her own which had been one of her mother's.

She put it on under a light cape and did not realise that, because her figure was so perfectly proportioned and her waist so tiny, she gave the gown, old though it might be, an elegance which was something that could not be purchased in any shop.

All the same, as they drove behind the four perfectly matched horses in the Marquis's well-sprung, comfortable carriage, Lara was aware that even beside Georgina she looked sadly out of place.

Georgina's gown was of fine muslin interspersed with little insets of lace and she wore with it a coat of satin trimmed with ermine at the cuffs.

It was just what Lara had dreamed of her heroine wearing and she thought it was a pity that Georgina was too young to play the lead in her story.

Nevertheless she made mental notes of the solicitous way in which the cockaded, top-hatted footman placed the rug over their knees, and the respectful manner in which the Butler and four footmen bowed them away from the door of Keyston House.

Nanny insisted that Lara should sit beside Georgina on the back seat of the carriage while she sat opposite them.

"I am sure as I am a stranger Georgina would rather have you next to her," Lara said.

She knew that Nanny was pleased at the suggestion. At the same time she replied:

"It's right for you to sit there, Miss Wade, and it's not something I intend to argue about!"

"Very well," Lara replied, "but I am quite prepared to change over at any time during the journey."

She found that her respectful manner and the flattery which she employed very skilfully had already softened Nanny's attitude towards her.

She guessed that in the past Governesses had tried to assert themselves and she remembered how her own Nanny had always been on the defensive with them.

'If I am to stay I must treat everybody in the same manner,' she told herself.

She set out to try to amuse Georgina, telling her stories, most of which she invented, about her own childhood and, aware that Nanny was listening, she was careful to say nothing that might make her presence seem suspicious.

Georgina grew tired before they finally reached the Priory, and as they turned in at the huge ornamental iron gates Nanny said:

"Now you'll go straight to bed, M'Lady. No hanging about, otherwise there'll be no riding tomorrow."

"I am going to ride tomorrow," Georgina said with a positive note in her voice that had not been there before. "I know *Snowball* will have missed me."

"Well, if you have a good rest tonight, we'll see about it," Nanny promised.

Lara noticed that Georgina looked sulky but there was undoubtedly a glint in her eyes.

This conversation told her that the child was keen

on riding, and she thought with a sudden excitement that, if Georgina rode, perhaps she also might be able to ride.

When Rollo was young she had ridden him every moment her father did not need him, but now the horse was growing old and it was almost a cruelty to take him far, or very fast.

Because the Vicarage was so far from anywhere, she longed to be able to ride every day, instead of having to walk over the fields and through the woods to the village.

Then she would pretend that she was on the back of a huge black stallion, or a snow-white Unicorn.

"Thank goodness we're home!" Nanny ejaculated.

Looking ahead of them down the long avenue of oak trees, Lara held her breath.

There had been so much she had to ask Jane so that she would not make a mistake once inside the Priory, that she had forgotten to ask her what it looked like outside.

Now as she saw it glowing like a jewel in the afternoon sun she thought it was the most beautiful house she had ever seen in her life.

She knew at once it was Elizabethan and must have been a Priory before the Dissolution of the Monasteries.

Built of red brick which had mellowed to a warm pink over the centuries, it was in the shape of an 'E' as a compliment to the Queen, and its gabled roofs, its tall twisting chimney-pots silhouetted against the sky, were lovelier than any building she had ever imagined in her dreams.

There was a wide stream running in front of it and a bridge, built at the same time as the house, to cross it.

Then there were smooth green lawns which looked like velvet, at the side of which the first spring shrubs were coming into blossom.

Almond trees edged the stream and yellow king-cups sloped down its banks into the water.

"It is lovely! Absolutely lovely!" Lara ejaculated, and did not realise she was speaking aloud.

"It's nice enough," Nanny said grudgingly, "and as I've said before, there's not place on earth that's perfect."

The way she spoke was so like her own Nanny that Lara could not help laughing.

Then as Nanny gave her a sharp glance she remembered that this was a very crucial moment.

After having come so far on her adventure, there was every chance she might be sent home ignominiously because Mr. Simpson, or perhaps the Marquis himself, did not think she was really necessary.

'Please, God, let me stay here,' she prayed.

She was still praying as she stepped out from the carriage after Georgina and went up the steps and in through the huge oak door surmounted by a coat-of-arms.

chapter three

LARA looked around the room and thought it was very comfortable and very luxurious for a School-Room, but at the same time rather badly arranged.

She had always had an artistic feeling for rooms, and she knew that if she stayed long she would have to move the sofa and tables around to make it more attractive.

However, as she was being very careful at the moment not to do anything wrong, she said nothing.

Mr. Simpson had accepted, without much comment, her explanation that she had come in Jane's place.

"I'm very sorry to hear that Miss Cooper's not well," he said, "but it was very considerate of her to send you in her place."

"I am an old friend," Lara replied, "and I have brought a reference in case you should need one."

She handed it across the desk to Mr. Simpson as she spoke, who looked at it perfunctorily, obviously not particularly interested.

She had written and signed it with her father's name, saying that Miss Wade had proved an excellent Governess in every way for his daughter and he was only too pleased to recommend her to any similar post.

Mr. Simpson had handed it back, saying:

"I hope you can persuade Lady Georgina to be a little more attentive to her lessons than she has been up until now. Every Governess we have had for her says the same: she finds lessons dull and will not concentrate."

Lara smiled.

"I think most children go through that phase at one time or another, and I understand that Lady Georgina's main interest is riding."

"That is true," Mr. Simpson agreed, "and her father was an exceptionally fine horseman, as is her uncle."

"You are very, very lucky to have good horses," Lara said in a soft voice.

She prayed as she spoke that Mr. Simpson would be perceptive enough to realise what she was hinting, and after a moment he said with a faint smile:

"You sound, Miss Wade, as if you would like to ride too."

Lara gave a little cry.

"Would it be possible? I cannot tell you how wonderful that would be for me! My life has been very restricted in the last few years because Lord Hurlington could not afford to keep many horses."

Mr. Simpson looked surprised. Then he said:

"I suppose, as Lord Hurlington is a Parson, that is understandable."

"I think you will find, Mr. Simpson," Lara replied, "that most Parsons are very badly paid."

Mr. Simpson laughed.

"There I can agree with you whole-heartedly, Miss Wade, because my father was one."

Lara felt she had found an ally when she least expected it.

"You will understand then," she said, "how wonderful it would be for me during the time I am here if I can ride with Lady Georgina."

"I will give orders to the stables that you can accompany her whenever she takes out her pony."

"Thank you, thank you," Lara cried, "and now I really feel as if I have stepped into a fairy-story."

It was a feeling that was accentuated when she went upstairs and saw the very comfortable suite of rooms which was allotted to Georgina and her Governess.

The child's bedroom was magnificent, and Lara's, although not quite so large, was a room she felt must have stepped out of one of her dreams.

But then the whole house was different from anything she had ever seen before, and the moment she awoke the following morning her one idea was to see everything she could of the Priory.

Georgina was obviously still tired and as it was not a particularly nice day, with grey skies overhead which hinted of rain, Nanny refused point-blank to allow her to ride.

Lara discovered that Nanny called Georgina in the morning, dressed her, and brought her into the School-Room for breakfast, then disappeared to her own rooms which she learned were like the Nurseries on another floor.

This answered one of the questions which had puzzled her: if Nanny was within hearing when Lord Magor called on Jane, why she did not interfere?

Now she realised that the School-Room had been brought down a floor from the Nurseries, and the suite which Georgina and her Governess occupied was isolated both from the grand rooms in the house and also from the Nursery and the servants' quarters.

'It is another case of being neither upstairs or downstairs,' Lara thought with a smile.

She had, however, been too busy to think of either Lord Magor or the Marquis because she wanted to concentrate on getting to know Georgina.

Having been told that she could not ride her pony that morning, Georgina looked sulky at breakfast and when it was over looked at Lara apprehensively as if she expected to be told that she had to do the lessons she disliked.

"What would you like to do?" Lara asked.

She saw the answer and prevented it from being said by adding quickly:

"Nanny said you cannot ride today, and it is just as disappointing for me as it is for you, because I am longing to ride with you, and I cannot tell you how excited and thrilled I am at the idea."

Georgina looked surprised.

"Can you ride, Miss Wade?" she asked. "None of my other Governesses has ever wanted to ride. They always want to drive about in the ponycart."

"I am certainly going to ride," Lara said, "and perhaps we could have races. I will give you a start as you are on a pony, but I am sure *Snowball,* although I have never seen him, is very fast."

"Very, very fast," Georgina answered proudly, "and I would like to race you, it will be fun!"

"Very well," Lara said. "That is what we will do tomorrow, but let us enjoy ourselves today and certainly not do any boring lessons."

She saw Georgina's eyes light up and she added:

"I think you must give me a lesson and show me round the house. That is if your uncle is out and we will not get in anybody's way."

"Uncle Ulric will have gone riding," Georgina said. "He always rides in the morning."

"What about his friends?"

"If there are ladies staying they will be in bed."

"Then perhaps we could see the rooms they will not be sitting in," Lara suggested.

She felt there were a dozen plots turning over in her mind in which the Priory would be the background.

As she and Georgina went downstairs she thought how grateful she was to Fate, or rather to Jane, who had given her this opportunity of seeing just the sort of house she needed for her novel.

They avoided the Main Hall, where she guessed there would be a number of footman on duty, and Georgina took her instead down another staircase.

This led to a wide corridor, hung with ancient armour and pictures of the Priors who ruled over the Priory before it was closed by the order of Henry VIII.

Lara wanted to stop and look at each of them, but Georgina hurried her along, saying:

"I thought first you would like to see the Orangery. It is very pretty and there are some birds in it which Uncle Ulric had brought here from across the sea."

To say the Orangery was pretty was an understatement. It had obviously been added to the house a century or so later, but it seemed to blend in with the original building.

But what took Lara's breath away was the profusion of orchids which were growing in it.

She had never seen any orchids, but she had read about them, and now to be confronted with dozens of different specimens of all colours and all sizes was to know that here was another subject which would fill the pages of her novel.

Georgina, however, hurried her past the mauve orchids and a collection of little star-shaped ones which looked as if they had fallen out of the sky.

At the far end of the Orangery was an enormous cage filled with budgerigars, the little love-birds which Lara found almost as fascinating as the flowers.

"I come and feed them when I can," Georgina said, "but Miss Cooper will never come down here because she is frightened of meeting Uncle Ulric or that nasty old Lord Magor."

Lara was surprised that the child knew so much.

"Why is he nasty?" she asked.

"He pretends he comes up to the School-Room to see me," Georgina replied, "but all the time he is looking at Miss Cooper, and I know she is frightened of him."

Lara thought that children always knew more than one suspected they did, and feeling this was a subject that should not be pursued, she said:

"I love these birds, and I will bring you here as often as you like."

Georgina smiled at her and fed the birds with the seed which was kept near the cage. Then she said:

"What would you like to see next? The Armoury or the Library?"

"I want to see them both!" Lara answered and Georgina laughed.

As they walked back through the Orangery she told

Georgina a story that she remembered about orchids, and another one that she invented about a budgerigar who carried a message seeking help for the little girl to whom it belonged when she had fallen down a cliff.

"That was very clever!" Georgina exclaimed.

"Of course she had trained the budgerigar to do what she told it for some time," Lara said quickly. "He would fly up to the ceiling and when she whistled fly down again onto her shoulder."

"Do you think we could teach one of Uncle Ulric's budgerigars to do that with me?" Georgina asked wistfully.

"We could try," Lara answered, "but perhaps it would be wise to have one of your own in the School-Room. Then if it refused to obey, we could catch it more easily and put it back in its cage."

"We will do that, promise we will do that!" Georgina cried.

"I will ask Mr. Simpson if you can have one," Lara replied.

She felt that at least she had broken through the dull lethargy with which Georgina seemed to have contemplated life until now.

They went next to the Library, and Lara kept up the little girl's interest by suggesting they should find out if there was a book on birds and how to train them.

The Curator, who was an old man with grey hair, was surprised at their question.

Lara explained who she was and he said:

"Her Ladyship seldom pays me a visit, but now she has asked me for a special book I must obviously find it for her."

"I am sure you must also have some books on horse-racing," Lara said.

The old Curator smiled.

"His Lordship has bought every book on the subject for years, and I can supply you with some very interesting pictures of horses, starting of course with how the Arab strain was brought to England."

Lara looked around the tightly packed book-shelves of the huge Library with its balcony from where one could reach the top shelves by using a little spiral staircase which led up to it."

"I never believed there could be so many books packed into one place!" she said. "I want to read them all!"

The Curator laughed.

"In which case, Miss Wade, you will have to stay here for at least two or three hundred years!"

"I am quite prepared to do that," Lara answered, "as long as I can read every book I want to."

She thought Georgina was beginning to look bored and she said quickly:

"Please give us one of your nicest picture-books on horse-racing, and as I remember the story of how the first Arab stallion came to England I would like that too, so that I can read it to Her Ladyship."

The Curator fetched the books, then as he gave them to Lara he said:

"If you come back this afternoon, My Lady, I promise you I will have the book on birds for you, but I cannot put my hand on it right now."

Georgina did not answer, and as they went from the Library, Lara carrying the precious books, she said:

"I do not want a book on birds, I want a bird all to myself."

"I will talk to Mr. Simpson as soon as I can see him," Lara promised. "But, please, now show me some more rooms in this wonderful house."

They walked for some way down the long corridor, then Georgina opened a door and Lara found herself in the Great Hall.

She knew this was where the monks had seen those who came to them for help, both physical and spiritual.

She stared at the high-beamed ceiling, the long diamond-paned windows, and the magnificently carved mantelpiece, thinking she was seeing a part of history.

She felt as if she could almost step back into the past and would find herself with a ruffle round her neck, being a dutiful, admiring servant of Queen Elizabeth.

Then because she felt she must share her thoughts with Georgina she said:

"Can you imagine what it was like when the monks were here and the Prior, who was a very holy man, taught them how they must help and feed anyone who came to the door?"

"Did they do that?" Georgina asked.

"Beggars were never turned away and when the winters were hard and cold there would not only be human beings who were hungry, but birds, deer, hares, and rabbits. They all trusted the monks because they were holy and would not do them any harm."

"Then why do they not come here today?" Georgina asked.

"Because it is no longer a holy place," Lara replied, "and the animals know that by instinct."

She spoke softly, feeling she could almost see the monks like St. Francis with the animals and the birds clustered around them.

Then she started as a voice behind her asked:

"Can you be disparaging those who now live in the Priory?"

She turned round and saw advancing towards them,

from a different door than the one through which they had entered the Great Hall, a man who she knew immediately was the Marquis.

It was not only because he was smartly dressed in his white breeches and polished riding-boots, but also because he was tall, broad-shouldered, authoritative and, what Jane had omitted to tell her, extremely handsome.

At the same time, since his voice had been mocking and sarcastic and there were deep lines running from his nose to the corners of his mouth which made him look cynical, she could understand that he could be extremely frightening.

"Oh, it is you, Uncle Ulric!" Georgina exclaimed. "I thought you had gone riding."

"As it is raining heavily I have returned," the Marquis replied. "Good-morning, Georgina! I imagine this is one of your lessons, but who is teaching you?"

He looked at Lara as he spoke in a way which made her immediately conscious that the gown she was wearing was shabby and that her hair, instead of being brushed smoothly into place in a way she thought looked respectable, was curling somewhat riotously round her forehead and over her ears.

Because she knew she must explain her own presence, she curtsied and said:

"My name is Wade, My Lord, and as Miss Cooper is ill I have taken her place until she is well enough to return."

"Why was I not told about this?" the Marquis enquired.

Lara thought his voice was hard, as if he resented anything happening in the house without his being aware of it.

"I saw Mr. Simpson when we arrived yesterday,"

Lara replied, "and he agreed that Lady Georgina should continue her lessons, and it would be a mistake for them to be interrupted."

She thought the Marquis raised his eyebrows and she had the terrifying feeling that perhaps, just when she had felt sure that she could stay, he would send her away.

Because she could not bear to lose the Priory before she had seen hardly any of it and it was so important to her personally, she said impulsively without thinking:

"Oh, please, Your Lordhsip, let me stay with Lady Georgina. It is not only that I shall enjoy teaching her, but I am so entranced with this wonderful, wonderful house."

She thought the Marquis looked surprised, and he said:

"But judging from what I overheard, not so entranced with its present ownership!"

"I would not presume to criticise you personally, My Lord," Lara answered quickly. "I was merely trying to make Lady Georgina see a picture of what the Priory must have looked like when it was peopled by those who devoted their lives to God."

"And you think that a life of prayer is preferable to living in the world as it is and being part of it?"

As Lara could never resist an argument, she had no idea that her eyes sparkled as she replied:

"I think it is a question, My Lord, of doing what we are best suited to do in life. While I greatly admire those who dedicate themselves wholly to the service of God, I confess to wishing for myself a much wider and more eventful existence, limited, unfortunately, by my means."

The Marquis laughed and she thought it was a

different sound from what she had expected.

"You are certainly very eloquent on the subject, Miss Wade," he remarked, "and I am sure Georgina will benefit from your wisdom."

He spoke in a dry voice which did not make it sound exactly a compliment.

"Miss Wade is going to ride with me, Uncle Ulric," Georgina said suddenly, as if that was where her thoughts had been, "and we are going to race each other. We have taken books from the Library to read about horse-racing."

The Marquis looked surprised.

"This is certainly a new departure," he said. "Are you a horse-woman, Miss Wade?"

"I hope so, My Lord! I have ridden all my life, but again I could hardly compare the mounts I have had up to now with the horses I expect to find in your stables."

"I do not think you will be disappointed," he said. "Do you believe that racing will improve and broaden Georgina's mind?"

"I am sure it will," Lara answered. "At the same time it will give me an inexpressible delight which I cannot adequately express in words."

The Marquis smiled. Then he said:

"You had better take Miss Wade to the race-course, Georgina, when you wish to race. Do not forget the rabbit-holes in the Park can be very treacherous."

"I will remember that, Uncle Ulric."

"I shall be interested to hear of your progress."

Without saying any more the Marquis turned and walked from the hall, leaving Lara and Georgina staring after him.

The child drew in her breath before she said:

"You were not frightened of Uncle Ulric, so I was

60

not frightened either, and he was nicer than he usually is."

"It is always a mistake to be frightened of anyone," Lara said.

At the same time she could not help feeling she had encountered a typhoon which had, at the last moment, passed her by without sweeping her off her feet.

While she went on talking to Georgina her heart was singing.

The Marquis had not sent her away from the Priory and she could ride what she was certain would be the most outstanding horses in the country.

Then she thought it wise, because it was growing late in the morning, not to encounter any members of the house-party, and she took Georgina back to the School-Room where they pored over the books from the Library.

After luncheon, which was brought up from downstairs by two footmen who waited on them and was more delicious than any meal Lara had ever eaten before, Nanny came bustling into the School-Room to say that Georgina must lie down.

"We have done lots of things this morning, Nanny," Georgina said.

"Then the quicker you go to sleep the better," Nanny replied.

Lara was certain that she was jealous because the child had enjoyed herself and she said quickly:

"Please, tell me for how long she sleeps and if you think it will be all right for me to take a walk in the garden. I do not wish to do anything which is wrong."

Because Lara was asking her assistance, the frown between Nanny's eyes cleared as she said:

"No, it'll be quite all right for you to do that, Miss

Wade, but keep away from the lawns directly outside the windows where you can be seen. You have an hour in which to do what you wish."

"Thank you very much," Lara said. "You are quite certain there is nothing I can do for you?"

"No, nothing," Nanny replied, but it was obvious she was pleased to have been asked.

Lara went to her bedroom and picked up the bonnet which belonged to Jane, but then decided, as no one was going to see her she need put nothing on her head.

Unless it was very sunny she never wore a hat or bonnet at home. But she was well aware that ladies behaved with propriety and even if they were only going into their own gardens they covered their heads and wore gloves.

"But I am not a lady," she said with a smile. "I am just a Governess, and who cares what I do?"

She had a quick glance at herself in the mirror and realised that once again, although she had tidied it before luncheon, her hair was curling irrepressibly and she gave it a quick brush.

'Oh, dear,' she said to herself, 'it is very difficult to look like a prim and proper, nondescript Governess when I feel because everything is so exciting that I want to dance over the grass and fly into the sky!'

Nanny had told her where the garden-door was which would lead her into the woods.

She followed her directions and found herself in the woods which encircled the house, the majority of the trees being great oaks which must have been planted soon after the Priory was built.

Their branches stretched out protectively and in the soft moss under them were growing primroses, the first flowers of spring.

It was so lovely that once again Lara stepped into

one of her fairy-stories. This time she was picturing the goblins who hid in the trees in the wood and would often play mischievous pranks on the other unsuspecting inhabitants.

She walked on, climbing a little higher until the house lay below and she could see the stream beyond it and the Park beyond that.

The rain had left the grass and the leaves damp and bespattered and now as the sun came out the raindrops glowed iridescent, each one a tiny rainbow in itself.

'It is lovely! How could anyone who lives here fail to be happy?' Lara asked.

Then she remembered the cynical lines on the Marquis's face and the dry note in his voice, and thought that he was not a happy man. He seemed to look on life with a jaundiced eye and find it boring.

'I am sure he is very difficult,' Lara thought, 'and I can understand Jane being frightened of him.'

But for herself there was no reason to be afraid, for when Jane returned she would leave, and she would never see either the Marquis or the Priory again.

At the same time it was wonderful copy, although she could not quite decide whether she would make him the hero or the villain of her novel.

She had planned that her heroine, the little Cinderella Governess, who of couse was Jane, would marry a Duke.

'Perhaps he could come to stay in the house,' Lara thought, 'and he would perhaps meet her in the corridor and fall in love with her at first sight. Then he would save her from the villain—Lord Magor.'

'I must see His Lordship so that I can describe him exactly,' she told herself.

She found a little path running between the trees which obviously led back towards the house, and she thought that she should begin to retrace her steps so as to be in the School-Room waiting for Georgina when she had finished her rest.

After a while the trees gave way to shrubs of lilac and syringa that were just coming into bud, and she was thinking how romantic it would be in a few days, when she heard voices and stopped still.

There was the sound of a female voice, high and rather musical, then a man's.

They were not very near and Lara could not hear what they said, but she walked a few more steps, thinking that if they were guests at the Priory she would be careful to avoid them.

At the turn of the path she saw in front of her the back of what was obviously a Summer-House and realised that this was where the voices came from.

"You are looking very beautiful, Louise," the man said, his voice deep.

"Thank you, Freddy, you always say the right thing. At the same time I am feeling particularly melancholy."

"I presume you are worried about Ulric."

"Of course I am! I was sure I could keep him, but he is slipping away and soon I shall be just another of those women who belong to his . . . past!"

The woman's voice was pathetic, and there was a little pause before the man replied:

"How can I advise you? I have known Ulric for years and to say that he is unpredictable is, as you know, an understatement."

"I love him, Freddy! I love him madly, and I was so certain that he would never tire of me as he has of Alice, Gladys, and of course Charlotte."

"You are so lovely, Louise, that I cannot imagine how any man could ever tire of you. In fact I think you are being needlessly despondent in thinking that is what has happened where Ulric is concerned."

"I wish I could believe you! I wish I could think that we meant as much to each other today as we did six months ago, but if I am honest with myself I know that this is the last time I shall be invited to stay at the Priory."

"Nonsense! Nonsense!"

Lara realised she was eavesdropping. At the same time she found it fascinating, and while she had no doubt as to who the lady called Louise was in love with, she longed to know who she was, and who was Freddy, to whom she was speaking.

Then she knew that her mother would think it very reprehensible for her to go on listening to a conversation that was not meant for her ears.

Moving very carefully in case she should step on a stick and they would realise they were not alone, she slipped away through the shrubs, finding her way back to the house the way she had come from it.

As she went upstairs she thought there was no end to the excitements that were all around her.

It was almost as if Fate had presented her with, as a special present, a conversation she could put straight into her novel word for word.

As she reached the School-Room it was to find that Georgina was up and dressed.

"Where have you been?" she asked "I wanted you."

"I am sorry," Lara replied. "I went for a walk in the wood and it took longer than I expected."

"I hate walking!" Georgina said. "Miss Cooper used to make me walk when I wanted to ride."

"I'm not allowing you to ride, so there's no use whining about it!" Nanny said. "At the same time, a breath of fresh air would do you good."

She picked up a light summer coat which was lying on the sofa.

"I have an idea," Lara said. "Nanny is quite right in saying you must not ride when you are tired, but I am sure you would like to show me *Snowball* and we could go and look at him in the stables. There would be no harm in that, would there, Nanny?"

Because her approval had been asked, Nanny was prepared to be conciliatory.

"No, but don't stay out too long," she answered.

"We will not do that," Lara promised, "and I will just go and fetch my bonnet."

She went quickly to her bedroom, and as she opened a drawer to take out her gloves she saw her notebooks lying there.

'I must remember every word,' she thought.

Then she and Georgina went down the stairs which led out of the back of the Priory towards the stables.

"I have slept today," Georgina said, "and it would not tire me to ride this afternoon."

"You will ride first thing tomorrow morning," Lara replied, "and I want you to choose which horse you think I should ride."

This gave the child a new interest, and she forgot for the moment that she had not been allowed to ride today.

The stables were just as marvellous as Lara had expected them to be and the horses even more magnificent.

She went from stall to stall, running out of adjectives with which to praise them, and delighted the Head Groom by her appreciation of everything he showed her.

She had no idea how lovely she looked with the flush on her cheeks and her eyes shining, her red hair glinting from under the small straw bonnet.

"How could anybody be so lucky as to own such finely bred horses?" she asked with a rapt note in her voice which the Head Groom did not miss.

"'is Lordship be a fine judge o' 'orseflesh, Miss," he replied. "Oi'll show ye the stallion 'e bought last month at Tattersall's. It be one o' the best thoroughbreds we've ever 'ad in the stables."

The stallion was, Lara thought, the double of the one which in her imagination had carried her over the fields at home. She therefore could not help herself asking:

"Do you think...would it be possible for...me to ride him?"

The Head Groom looked doubtful.

"Oi'd 'ave to ask 'is Lordship about that."

"Yes, of course, and I am sure he will not trust me with a new acquisition which must be very precious to him."

"Most o' the young ladies as rides 'ere," the Head Groom answered, "don't very often call at the stables, an' when they does they're afraid of anythin' as pulls, or is too spirited."

"But that is what I like, and have always longed for," Lara said. "So please choose me a spirited horse that I can ride tomorrow morning."

The Head Groom laughed and, although she could not ride *Black Knight*, as the stallion was called, he showed her a horse called *Glorious*, which she agreed was a very adequate substitute.

When they went back to the house after she had seen *Snowball* and understood why Georgina loved him, she said:

"I wonder if you realise how lucky you are. When I was young I had just a donkey to ride until he died.

Then I shared a horse with my mother which when he grew old we could not afford to replace."

"Were you very poor?" Georgina asked interestedly.

"Yes, very," Lara answered.

The child was silent for a moment. Then she said:

"It does not seem fair, does it, that Uncle Ulric should have dozens of horses, and although you love them just as much as he does, you do not possess one."

"I would like to be as lucky as that," Lara agreed, "but we all have compensations of some sort. I mean, though I cannot own horses, I have something that your uncle has not got."

"What is that?" Georgina asked curiously.

"I think you would call it 'imagination,'" Lara replied, following the train of her thoughts. "When I cannot have something like that stallion, I imagine it, and in that way he belongs to me and nobody can take him away from me."

Georgina clapped her hands.

"That is a lovely idea! Let us imagine all the things we can have which Nanny cannot say are too much for me, or which Uncle Ulric can refuse to buy me."

"Now you start," Lara said. "What do you want?"

There was a pause. Then Georgina said:

"I would like to have a Band all to myself, because when they come to play at the parties Nanny always takes me away to bed and I am not allowed to listen to them."

"So you like music?" Lara said.

"Sometimes I hear it in my head."

"Now I think of it," Lara remarked, "you have no piano in the School-Room."

She thought as she spoke it was strange because

she always imagined that every child like herself would be taught music.

"We had one once, a long time ago," Georgina replied, "but Nanny said that the noise gave her a headache, and the Governess who was with me then would only let me play scales, which I got awfully bored with."

There was something in the way she spoke about music with a touch of enthusiasm in her voice which was the same as when she spoke about riding.

"There must be a piano somewhere in the house," Lara remarked.

"There is one in the Music-Room," Georgina replied, "but Miss Cooper would never go down there."

Lara remembered that Jane, with all her intelligence, had never been musical. In fact she doubted if she could play the piano at all.

They went in through a side door, but instead of going straight upstairs Lara asked:

"Will you show me the Music-Room? There is not likely to be anybody about at this time of the day."

"Would you really like to see it?" Georgina enquired.

"Very much!" Lara answered.

The child led her down into the same corridor where the Library was situated, but now they went along towards the West Wing of the house, and Georgina opened the door of what Lara thought must be the perfect Music-Room.

It had obviously been added much later to the original Monastery, oval in shape with pillars at both ends. A magnificent Broadwood piano stood in a centre alcove on a raised dais.

Lara drew in her breath.

The very old upright piano at the Vicarage was

always going out of tune, and the ivory keys were yellow with age.

She walked towards the Broadwood, opened the lid, and sat down on the piano-stool.

"Are you going to play something?" Georgina asked in a rapt little voice.

"Listen to this," Lara replied, "then tell me what sort of music you like."

She played first part of a Sonata by Chopin, then without stopping followed it with a Strauss Waltz.

She realised as she played that Georgina was watching her, listening with an almost ecstatic expression on her face.

'The child is musical!' Lara thought to herself.

She decided this must be the key to Georgina's indifference to everything around her, and her lack of interest in any of her lessons.

She had learnt from her reading that real musicians were often moody and melancholy when they were children and seemed detached from their surroundings simply because they could not be fed mentally with the music their whole character and personality craved.

As she finished playing, she rose from the piano-stool and said:

"Now you try."

Georgina looked at her in surprise.

"I cannot play like you. Play something else."

"No," Lara said. "I want you to show me what you can do."

"I have only learnt scales."

"Never mind. Remember what I have just played to you, and see if you can play the time with one finger."

For a moment Georgina sat staring blankly at the key-board.

Then as if her small hands were drawn irresistibly towards the notes she touched them gently, one by one, until as Lara held her breath she began to pick out note by note what she could hear in her mind.

Then she looked up at Lara with a smile on her face.

"I can do it!"

"Of course you can," Lara answered. "And now, Georgina, we are going to have music lessons every day as long as I am here."

The child stared at her as if she could not believe what she had heard. Then she asked:

"Real lessons like this?"

"Yes, exactly," Lara answered, "and I promise you that in a few weeks you will be able to play just as well, if not better, than I do."

Georgina gave a cry of delight that was somehow very pathetic. Then she said:

"Teach me, please teach me. I want to play just like you, and it will be as exciting as riding."

They stayed in the Music-Room for nearly an hour. Then Lara thought guiltily that Nanny would be angry because they were late for tea.

"We must go back to the School-Room now," she said, "and I think, Georgina, we will keep the lessons as a secret for the moment, until you can surprise everybody by showing them how well you can play."

"I will tell nobody, not even Nanny," Georgina said, "because she does not like music."

"It will be our secret," Lara repeated.

Georgina touched the ivory keys just once more, as if she were saying good-night to them.

Lara shut the lid of the piano and they walked out of the Music-Room and back along the passage.

They had almost reached the staircase which would lead them up to the School-Room without going through the main Hall when coming towards them Lara saw a man.

He was obviously a guest and her first instinct was to turn round and go in the opposite direction.

Then she thought it would be a mistake for Georgina to think they must be too surreptitious about what they had been doing, and she walked on.

The man was rather heavily built, and as they drew nearer she saw that he was handsome in a rather heavy manner, with dark eyes and hair just beginning to grey at the temples.

As she was watching him she felt Georgina's hand slip into hers, and without there being any need for anybody to tell her who he was, she knew instinctively she was about to meet Lord Magor.

chapter four

RIDING over the Park on *Glorious* with Georgina beside her on *Snowball*, Lara thought she had never been so happy.

It was an indescribable delight to ride the most magnificent horse she had ever been on, and she could see the beauty of the Priory on one side of her, and the ancient oaks and the spotted deer beneath them on the other.

Once again she felt she had stepped into one of her dreams, and she must try to remember every moment of it before she woke up.

Last night when she went to bed she had thanked God for the unexpected happiness that had come into her life.

At the same time she had a feeling of triumph because she had met Lord Magor and had not been afraid of him.

He was, however, exactly like she had expected the villain in one of her stories to be.

When he saw Georgina he had put out his hand to say:

"Good-afternoon, little lady. And how are you to-day?"

Lara felt Georgina shrink a little nearer to her before she replied:

"Quite well...thank you."

She had ignored his outstretched hand and Lord Magor looked at Lara with a quizzical expression on his face.

"And who is this?" he asked. "And what has happened to Miss Cooper?"

Knowing Georgina had no wish to answer him, Lara had dropped a small curtsy before she replied:

"I am Miss Wade, My Lord, and I have taken Miss Cooper's place temporarily because she is ill."

"Ill?" Lord Magor exclaimed. "I am sorry to hear that."

He did not, however, sound very sorry. He was looking at her in a way that she instinctively resented, feeling he appraised her as he would have a horse.

There was also an expression in his eyes with which he would not have regarded a horse, and she was sure it would have frightened poor Jane.

"Please excuse us, My Lord," she said, "or we will be late for tea."

Lord Magor smiled and she thought the curve of his lips was unpleasant.

"You sound very strict, Miss Wade, and I hope you are not too severe as a teacher to dear little Georgina."

"I think she is quite content with the lessons I am

giving her, My Lord," Lara replied. "Good-after-noon."

She walked away before he could answer, knowing Georgina was only too eager to leave him.

She did not look back. But she had the feeling that he had not moved from where he was standing, and was watching them walk down the corridor until they were out of sight.

"I hate Lord Magor!" Georgina said when she knew he could not hear her.

"Then we must just try to avoid him," Lara answered.

She could understand easily that he was the type of man who would make Jane feel defenceless and unable to face him.

It was utterly despicable for a man in his position to pursue a young Governess who was afraid of losing her job if she complained.

'I wish I could hurt him,' Lara thought.

It was, however, unlikely that he would wish to run after her in Jane's absence. At the same time, inexperienced though Lara was with men, she knew that when he looked at her she felt uncomfortable.

When the footman removed her supper and said good-night, Lara had waited until she heard him going down the stairs, then had firmly locked herself in behind the School-Room door.

She had ascertained earlier in the day that there was a strong lock on it and wondered why Jane, who admitted to having locked herself in her bedroom, had not locked the outer door as well.

But Jane, sweet though she was, was rather silly, and despite her resolution to teach Lord Magor a lesson Lara had no intention of being put at a disadvantage until the right moment came to confront him.

Dismissing Lord Magor from her thoughts, she concentrated on riding Glorious until they moved out of the Park and passed the end of a thick wood to arrive at the race-course.

Lara had expected when the Marquis referred to it that it would be just a flat field with perhaps some artificial jumps.

What she had not anticipated was that it would be constructed exactly like a real race-course, oval in shape with railings running all round it.

At the moment there were no fences, but she could see them stacked outside the railings ready to be set up should they be required.

"What a splendid place to gallop!" she exclaimed.

Georgina looked at her questioningly.

"When I come here with a groom," she said, "I am only allowed to gallop on a leading-rein."

"I have watched you riding," Lara said, "and I think you are quite capable of managing by yourself."

"Of course I am!" Georgina declared. "And if I am to race you, I have to be on my own."

"Yes, but I think I had better give you a start because *Glorious* is so much bigger than *Snowball*."

As Lara spoke she saw a horse emerge from an entrance into the wood, and was aware that the Marquis was coming towards them.

"There is Uncle Ulric!" Georgina exclaimed, and she did not sound pleased.

Lara did not reply. She only waited until the Marquis, riding *Black Knight,* came to a stand-still beside them.

"Good-morning, Georgina," he said. "Good-morning, Miss Wade. What do you think of my race-course?"

"I am very impressed with it," Lara answered, "and

Georgina and I are just about to race each other."

She spoke a little defiantly, as if she felt he might stop them, but the Marquis replied:

"A good idea! And as I see you are riding *Glorious,* I think I might try out his paces against *Black Knight's.*"

Georgina looked apprehensively at him as she asked:

"Are you saying you are going to race with us, Uncle Ulric?"

"Why not?" the Marquis enquired. "But *Snowball* must certainly have a chance of winning and I suggest you start where that post is at the turn of the course."

He pointed it out as he spoke and Lara was aware it was nearly half-way to the winning-post, which was clearly marked near where they were standing at the moment.

Georgina's eyes had lit up and she looked pretty and alert as she replied:

"I will take *Snowball* there now, Uncle Ulric. How will I know when we have to start?"

"I will say: 'One, Two, Three—Go!'" the Marquis replied. "And I will make certain you will hear me."

Georgina glanced at Lara with an excited smile and rode off, looking very attractive on her white pony in a pretty summer habit of pale pink cotton.

Because she was thinking of how attractive the child looked, Lara was suddenly conscious of her own appearance.

She was wearing a black habit that had belonged to her mother.

It had once been comparatively expensive and was well cut, but since Lady Hurlington had worn it for many years and so had Lara, it was now threadbare at the seams.

Although the white muslin blouse she wore under

it was crisp and clean, she could not pretend that she looked at all smart or could possibly compare with the elegance of the women with whom the Marquis usually rode.

What was more, because she never wore one at home except for special occasions, she had no hat on her head.

She had expected, as she and Georgina were out so early, that nobody would see them, and she had merely rolled her hair into a chignon at the back of her neck and brushed it as tidily as she could in front.

She was well aware, however, that there were already little curls escaping as they always did round her forehead, and she wondered if the Marquis was shocked that a Governess should be so casually dressed and certainly not showing a good example to her pupil.

Then, as if he knew what she was thinking, he said dryly:

"You look slightly unconventional, Miss Wade. At the same time, I can see you know how to sit a horse."

"I shall be very upset if after this morning you do not think I am good enough to ride the magnificent horses in your stable, My Lord."

"I think that is unlikely," the Marquis replied, "but of course we shall know by the end of the race."

It was as if he challenged her in more ways than one, and Lara had the feeling he was being deliberately provocative as if by making her nervous he would gain an easy victory.

Then she told herself it was presumptuous of her to think he was considering her feelings in any way and was concerned about anything except her position as Georgina's teacher.

The child had by this time reached the place that

the Marquis had pointed out. She waved her hand and he acknowledged it by raising his.

Then he said:

"I imagine you will also expect a small start, Miss Wade, as *Black Knight* is definitely faster than *Glorious*."

"I expect you to be fair, My Lord, with anything that is concerned with sport."

She thought there was a twist to the Marquis's lips, as if he appreciated that she had singled out something that was undeniably true while leaving a question-mark over other aspects of his life.

Then, afraid she had been too outspoken, she moved *Glorious* forward, saying:

"Please tell me, My Lord, when I am to stop."

She had not gone very far before he said:

"I think that is far enough, and now, if you are ready . . ."

He looked towards Georgina, then clearly, his voice ringing out as he counted to three, he ended with a loud:"Go!"

Lara saw that Georgina had in fact started *Snowball* off as soon as the Marquis began to count, and with difficulty she restrained *Glorious* until the final word.

It was obviously not the first time *Glorious* had raced, and he leaped forward, accelerating at the first sound of *Black Knight* coming up behind him.

The course was as long as a regular public race-course and Lara at first kept *Glorious* on a tight rein, determined if she possibly could to beat the Marquis.

She knew he was gaining on her and she found it was not just a question of the supremacy of their horses but of themselves and their personalities.

She could not explain exactly why she thought this. She only knew that because he was so authoritative and obviously contemptuous of those around him, she desperately wanted to beat him.

She wanted to show that he could not be the winner over everybody, especially herself.

The Marquis had, Lara realised, been clever in allotting Georgina a place on the course which kept her out of the way of their horses and made it possible for *Snowball* to win.

The child did in fact pass the winning-post just two seconds before she and the Marquis, galloping neck and neck down the straight, reached it.

For one moment Lara thought she had won, then with what she knew was superb horsemanship he passed the post just ahead of her.

It took a little time to draw in *Black Knight* and *Glorious* and as they turned round to ride back towards Georgina the little girl was shouting with excitement.

"I won! I won! Did you see me win, Miss Wade?"

"I saw you. You rode very well," Lara replied.

She spoke breathlessly because she was still unable to breathe normally after so much exertion.

"Uncle Ulric was second," Georgina said as they rode up to her.

"And I was last," Lara said with a smile, "but *Glorious* certainly did his best."

She bent forward to pat her horse on the neck as she spoke and the Marquis said:

"And so did you, Miss Wade. I think this is a lesson in which Georgina has a most proficient teacher."

"Thank you, My Lord," Lara replied. "That is certainly a compliment I appreciate."

"I am stating a fact, Miss Wade!" the Marquis corrected.

He spoke in his usual dry voice, and it seemed to

Lara that his eyes rested on her untidy hair and her threadbare habit.

She could almost read the thoughts with which he was criticising her, and her chin went up defiantly as she said:

"Thank you, My Lord, for a most unforgettable experience."

Then she deliberately rode away from him to say to Georgina:

"I think now we should ride home, or Nanny will think you have exerted yourself too much on your first day of riding after being ill."

"I am not tired, and Nanny is an old fuss-pot!" Georgina remarked.

"Nevertheless, we must do what she says," Lara said. "Thank your uncle for letting you race with him and then perhaps you can take me home a different way. I would love to see the wood."

She knew there was a path from which the Marquis had appeared.

Obediently Georgina looked at her uncle.

"Thank you, Uncle Ulric."

"We must race again another day," the Marquis replied.

Georgina's eyes lit up.

"Tomorrow?" she questioned.

"I am leaving this afternoon for London," the Marquis replied, "but I shall be back next Friday, and we must try to arrange something then."

"Perhaps we can go round the course twice," Georgina suggested hopefully.

"That will be up to Miss Wade," the Marquis answered.

He looked at Lara as he spoke, touched his hat, and as he rode away from them, Lara could not fail to notice how magnificent he looked astride the big black stallion.

The Head Groom had been right in saying he was an exceptional rider, and she thought almost despondently that however hard she tried she would never be able to win a race against him.

"Uncle Ulric was much nicer than he usually is," Georgina was saying. "And he did not seem to notice that I was riding without a leading-rein."

"I know," Lara said. "And you will never need to use one again."

"You must tell the grooms that in the stables," Georgina said. "Otherwise when you have left they will make me ride beside them and will not listen when I say I can ride by myself."

"I will tell the Head Groom," Lara promised.

At the same time she thought that when she did leave she would try to make the Marquis give the order so that there would be no misunderstanding.

She wondered if he was at all interested in his niece, and in an effort to find out she said to Georgina as they walked their horses towards the wood:

"I am sure your uncle was very proud to see how well you could ride."

Georgina did not answer and Lara asked:

"Do you not think he was?"

"Uncle Ulric is not interested in me," Georgina said, "except that he is very, very glad I am not a boy!"

Lara was startled.

"What do you mean by that?" she asked.

"If I were a boy, I would have become the Marquis when Papa died," Georgina replied. "Papa was always very angry that I was not the son he expected me to be, so nobody really wants me."

Lara was at first surprised at what Georgina said, but she realised that the child was not speaking pathetically in order to win sympathy, but was just stating a fact.

"I am sure that is not true," she said quickly.

"Yes, it is," Georgina answered. "If I had been a boy I would have been called George, like all the eldest sons in the family, and I have heard the servants say that Mama prayed and prayed that she would have a son, and when they told her I was a girl she cried."

Lara thought that servants always talked irresponsibly in front of children.

She could understand that Georgina would think over what she had heard and this, besides the fact that she was starved of music, would make her lethargic and uninterested in what was going on around her.

Aloud she said:

"Well, I think you are very lucky. I would much rather be a woman than a man."

"Why?" Georgina asked.

"Because men have to go to wars and fight as soldiers, or if they are poor they have to work very hard to keep their wives and families. You are a woman, so all that is done for you."

Georgina thought this over for a moment. Then she said:

"But you have to work, and so does Miss Cooper."

Lara thought the child was far more intelligent than anybody gave her credit for, and she replied:

"The reason my father is not a rich man is that he is a Parson, and he spends his life in worshipping God and helping other people."

Georgina was interested.

"Does your father like being a Parson, even though it makes him poor?"

"It is what he always wanted to be," Lara explained, "and when you are doing what you want to do, it is a happiness which outweights being rich or owning a lot of possessions."

"I want to ride."

"I know," Lara said, "and you are very lucky that you have someone to provide you with fine horses. Otherwise you would have to work very hard to buy one for yourself."

Georgina laughed as if this was a funny idea. Then she said:

"What could I do to earn money?"

"Luckily that is something that is not likely to occur in your life," Lara said. "At the same time, I am almost sure, Georgina, that if you work at your music, you would be able to earn a living that way."

The child looked at her with excitement in her eyes. Then she said:

"If I could earn money by playing, that means I will have to be very good."

"Very, very good," Lara answered. "And that is what I think you will be if you try hard enough."

In the wood the path was not wide enough for them to ride side by side, and as Georgina went ahead to lead the way Lara was certain she was thinking seriously about what she was being told, and it would make her even keener than she was already to play the piano.

'Perhaps I am wrong in telling her so,' she thought, 'but I feel certain she has an unusual talent that should be cultivated and it will be sad if, when I leave, she is not allowed to continue with her music lessons."

She thought this was another matter about which she should speak to the Marquis and that she would be more aware of Georgina's possibilities by the time he returned from London.

It was a joy to think that Lord Magor would also be leaving, and at least she would not have to worry about him until next Saturday.

As if thinking of him conjured him up in person, when they reached the house and left their horses with a groom who was waiting outside the front door, Lord Magor appeared at the top of the steps.

He was dressed smartly in clothes which told Lara he was going to London with the Marquis.

As she and Georgina walked up the steps towards him, she knew he was looking at her and there was certainly no criticism in his eyes such as she thought there had been in the Marquis's.

Instead she knew that her hair glinting in the sunshine against her white skin, which was thrown into prominence by the darkness of her habit, was making him look at her with admiration, but there was definitely something unpleasant about it.

"Good-morning, little lady!" Lord Magor said in his over-mellow voice to Georgina. "And how are you this morning? Have you enjoyed your ride?"

"Yes, thank you," Georgina replied.

"And you, Miss Wade," Lord Magor went on, "you look like Diana the Huntress and just as beautiful as her picture in the Louvre."

Lara had reached the top of the steps by now and as Lord Magor spoke she merely inclined her head in acknowledgment.

Then, as she went to pass him, Georgina having already run ahead, he said in a low voice that only she could hear:

"And that is a picture I would like to show you one day!"

For a moment Lara felt she could not have heard him aright. But as she would have entered the Hall he put out his hand to prevent her from doing so.

"You will be here next week?" he asked.

As he touched her Lara stiffened, then replied:

"I may be, My Lord, but now excuse me, for I must take Georgina upstairs."

She moved her arm away from his hand and walked quickly away with her head held high to join Georgina, who was already climbing the stairs.

As she did so she heard Lord Magor laugh softly, and it was the laugh of a man, she thought, who had seen something he wanted and was quite determined to get it.

It was later in the day, when she had learnt from Nanny that the Marquis and his guests had all gone, that she told herself she must have been mistaken in what Lord Magor said, and was merely weaving tales about him because she had cast him as the villain in her book.

"His Lordship," she said to Nanny, "will not return until next Friday. Will there be another party?"

"I expect so," Nanny replied. "The house is always full of people, but we sees little of them, since no one wants Her Ladyship downstairs, as is right and proper."

Lara made no comment on this for a moment. Then she asked tentatively:

"Perhaps some of His Lordship's friends would like to see Georgina. Is it not a mistake for her always to remain up here?"

Nanny made a sound which was definitely a snort of indignation.

"I know what's right," she said. "The ladies who stay here are busy ingratiating themselves with His Lordship. All they thinks about is their faces!"

"I have always heard about what are called the Professional Beauties," Lara said, "but I have never had the opportunity of seeing any of them."

"You'll see them if you stays here long enough," Nanny replied, "but it won't do you any good."

There was no doubt of the scorn in her voice, and Lara said:

"Tell me who was here at this last party, in case I have ever read about them in the newspapers or magazines."

She thought for a moment that Nanny was going to refuse. Then she reeled off names which were more or less familiar:

"The Countess de Grey, the Marchioness of Downshire, Lady Louise Lesley."

At the last name Lara started and knew that this was what she wanted to hear.

"I have heard of the first two ladies," she said, "and I know Lady de Grey is a so-called Professional Beauty. But who is Lady Louise Lesley?"

"Just another conceited little Madam with her eyes on His Lordship!" Nanny replied tartly. "She's lasted longer than most of them, but she'll get her wings singed, they all do!"

Her tone was so scathing that Lara had to laugh and she said:

"She is obviously in your 'black books.'"

"That's a fact," Nanny replied. "I don't hold with any of the goings-on in the Social World! That poor beautiful Princess Alexandra has to put up with the Prince of Wales's carryings-on, and it's not surprising the Queen disapproves!"

Even in Little Fladbury it was known how much the Queen disliked her son's friends and the Marlborough House Set.

Lara thought with amusement there must be Nannies all over the world saying what was obviously echoed by the more strait-laced members of the population, whose opinions were often expressed in the newspapers.

Because she felt she must support the Prince of Wales she said:

"I expect because he is still a comparatively young man, he finds the gloom of Windsor Castle very dreary."

"Dreary or not, the Queen rules over us and has to be obeyed," Nanny replied. "It's a great mistake for anybody to think they can do otherwise."

As if she had nothing further to add to the conversation, she picked up the roll of crochet-lace she was making and which she always carried about with her and left the School-Room.

Lara, however, had found out what she wanted to know.

When later in the evening Agnes, the maid who looked after her, was turning down her bed she said:

"Do tell me, Agnes, has Lady Louise Lesley very pretty gowns?"

"Oo, they're lovely, Miss!" Agnes exclaimed. "I've helped her lady's-maid to iron some of them, and you'd never believe how skilfully they're made, all embroidered with pearls and diamonds too."

"And is she very beautiful?" Lara enquired.

"His Lordship thinks so, and so do we. She's been here a lot."

"Do you think she will marry the Marquis?"

Agnes looked at her in surprise.

"She can't do that, Miss. Lord Lesley comes with her sometimes, but he's often in Scotland for the fishing."

"She is . . . married!" Lara exclaimed.

Then she thought how very silly she had been to imagine on overhearing the conversation between Lady Louise and Lord Magor that there was any possibility of her marrying the Marquis.

She had begun to weave her into the story as the girl who longed for him to offer her a wedding-ring, but he had eluded her just when she thought she had captured him.

Instead it had been a *liaison* such as she had read about in novels, and Lady Louise was the villainess, a woman who was unfaithful to her husband!

She was certainly to be condemned, and rightly so, by Nanny and those who listened to her father's sermons.

Somehow, because the Marquis had seemed so cynical and aloof, she had never thought of him as being the passionate, ardent lover she intended to describe in her books as the hero.

She could not forget how sad and pathetic Lady Louise had sounded as she said:

"'I was sure I could keep him, but he is slipping away and soon I shall just be another of those women who belong to his . . . past.'"

How could she have said that when she already had a husband? And were the other women who had belonged to the Marquis also married?

Almost as if she could hear Lady Louise speaking beside her, Lara heard her say:

"'. . . I was so certain he would never tire of me as he has of Alice, Gladys, and of course Charlotte.'"

Because she was silent Agnes looked at her a little apprehensively and said:

"P'raps I shouldn't have spoken as I did, Miss, but you did want to know."

"Yes, of course, Agnes," Lara replied. "I was just thinking about the parties that must take place here, and wishing I could see them."

"There'll be one next week-end, Miss," Agnes said, "and I'll show you how you can have a peep at the ladies going down to dinner. Ever so lovely they looks, and when the Prince of Wales comes to stay the gentlemen wear their decorations and they glitters too."

There was no doubt it was very exciting for Agnes and Lara said impulsively:

"I would love to see them!"

"You leave it to me, Miss," Agnes said, "But don't tell Nanny. She don't approve of the 'goings-on-downstairs,' as she calls them, but if you ask me, it's just jealousy!"

Lara laughed.

"I am not jealous, only very interested."

She thought as she spoke this was exactly what she wanted for her book. At the same time she knew because of what she had just learned that the plot was growing rather complicated.

'One thing is quite certain,' she thought, 'Lord Magor is indisputably the villain.'

Then she had the uncomfortable feeling that perhaps the Marquis was making a bid for that role. After all, there were Alice, Gladys, and Charlotte, not to mention Lady Louise, to prove his villainy!

* * *

The next day Lara thought the whole house seemed freer and happier once the Marquis had departed, and there was nobody occupying the important State Bed-rooms on the First Floor, while the Drawing-Rooms downstairs were also empty.

Georgina took her to see them and she found them

all beautiful, attractive, and filled with exquisite, fantastic, and attractive objets d'art.

"This is the Queen's Drawing-Room," Georgina answered.

Lara saw the room had pictures and relics which had belonged not only to Queen Elizabeth but other Queens who had stayed over the centuries at the Priory.

There were also the Garden-Room, the Blue Drawing-Room, the Silver Salon which had been added later, and there was a Ball-Room which Lara found breath-taking.

Beside these there were a number of other rooms each more beautiful than the last, and a Chapel.

The Chapel, which was Elizabethan, had its original carved pews and a magnificent gold reredos which the Curator told her had been found after lying hidden for two hundred years in the cellars beneath the house.

It was very impressive and to Lara it had an atmosphere of sanctity and peace.

When the Curator and Georgina had moved away to look at something else, she knelt down and said a prayer of gratitude. She also asked for help in developing a talent in Georgina which she knew had been hidden from everyone else.

"Help me, God, to make her happy," she prayed.

Then almost as if seeing his face in front of her eyes she found herself praying that the Marquis would be happy too.

She did not know why she was so conscious of him as a person, and it was difficult to think how with such possessions any man could be anything but elated and joyful since life had been so bountiful to him.

'What has upset him?' she wondered, then told herself it was none of her business.

It was only because the Marquis was so different from any man she had ever seen or imagined that she found herself continually thinking about him.

The days passed quickly and every time she took Georgina to the Music-Room she became more and more convinced that the child had an extraordinary aptitude for music.

In a few days she was able to pick out by ear anything Lara played.

Lara was sure too that her touch on the keys and the way she moved her hands proclaimed, if nothing else, that music was part of her whole make-up, and it was only a question of teaching and bringing out the instinct which was already there.

Then Lara thought a little helplessly that it would be a very difficult thing to explain.

If, as Georgina thought, her uncle was not interested in her, how could she be sure that when she left, the child would have the best teachers and a chance of becoming, if not a musical genius, a very competent performer?

"I will make him understand," she determined and found herself trying to play her very best so that she could set Georgina a standard to follow.

They rode every morning, which was an inexpressible delight, and Lara soon began to know her way through the woods and the fields that lay round the house.

Then they explored a little further and Lara saw how excellently farmed the land was and how attractive the farm buildings themselves were which looked as if they had stepped out of a picture-book.

They rode through thick forests of firs, stopped beside streams which ran through lush meadows, and then found little hamlets where there were the inevitable ancient Inn, village green, and duck-pond.

She found there was so much to do, so many people she wanted to see and talk to, that the days flew by. When she went to bed at night it was to sleep as soon as her head touched the pillow.

It was almost a shock when Agnes said:

"His Lordship'll be back tonight, Miss, and have you heard who's coming tomorrow?"

"No, I've not," Lara replied.

"I s'pose Nanny wouldn't tell you," Agnes said, "but it's the Prince of Wales!"

"He is coming here?" Lara exclaimed.

"Yes, Miss, and of course his friend, Lady Brooke, is coming too."

Lara's eyes widened.

She had read about Lady Brooke because she was featured frequently in the *'Ladies Journal,'* which Lara often saw because a woman in the village kindly lent it to her.

It had described the beauty and wealth of Lady Brooke, who had married the eldest son of the Earl of Warwick, and there were sketches of her and her elaborate gowns in almost every issue.

Lara could not believe what Agnes seemed to be insinuating, and as if she saw that she looked bewildered, the housemaid said in a low voice:

"Everyone knows, Miss, that the Prince is madly in love with Her Ladyship. Her travels everywhere with him in his special train and he's always staying at Easton Lodge."

"So he is . . . in love with . . . her!" Lara said in a strange voice.

"Oh yes, Miss. His Lordship's valet says the Prince can't take his eyes off her, and the house-parties Her Ladyship gives for His Royal Highness have all the

Prince's friends at them, like His Lordship."

Until now the newspapers had always coupled the Prince's name with the beautiful Lily Langtry and it struck Lara that the gentlemen of the Marlborough House Set were always changing their affections and she supposed they and the Marquis were only following the Royal example.

She thought it was indiscreet to say so to Agnes. At the same time because for the sake of her book she wanted to know more, she asked:

"Is Lady Brooke the most beautiful woman who ever comes here?"

"Well, that's hard to say, Miss," Agnes replied. "His Lordship's ladies are all dazzling, you might say, but Lady Brooke's every so sweet and nice. Everyone in the house admires her."

She gave a little laugh and added:

"Just like His Royal Highness!"

Lara could not help thinking that her mother would disapprove of this conversation, but still she had to know more.

"Will Lady Louise be coming this week-end?" she asked.

Agnes shook her head.

"I'm not sure, Miss. But I will know as soon as Mr. Simpson gives Mrs. Blossom the Housekeeper the bedroom list."

The next afternoon Lara could not help asking Agnes who was on the list and she reeled off a lot of names, some of which Lara thought she had heard of, and some of which were unknown to her. But one was not surprising, and that was Lord Magor.

"Does Lord Magor have a special lady-friend?" she asked.

Agnes shrugged her shoulders.

"If you asks me, Miss, His Lordship just enjoys being such a close friend of the Master. He seems to fit into every party, so to speak."

This seemed incomprehensible to Lara; for if Lord Magor had the choice of so many beauties, why should he be interested in poor Jane and perhaps herself?

Then she wondered if perhaps it was because he liked woman who were not as sophisticated as were the guests in the house-party.

"Every man has his own interests," she had heard her father say once.

'Perhaps,' she ruminated, 'because he is so over-powering and unpleasant he likes women who are timid and frightened of him, which certainly none of the great beauties like Lady Brooke or Lady de Grey are likely to be.'

All the same it was all very difficult to understand, but at the same time fascinating.

Lara was, however, determined to make quite certain the School-Room door was locked! Or was she perhaps being presumptuous in thinking that Lord Magor was really interested in her?

*   *   *

At five o'clock that evening the whole house seemed to come alive and buzz like bees in a hive.

There were housemaids everywhere, preparing the bedrooms, although they had all been cleaned every day since the previous week.

There were footmen in livery waiting in the Hall, their silver buttons polished until they shone blindingly.

Mrs. Blossom the Housekeeper, with a silver chatelaine clinking from her waist, was inspecting the rooms and finding fault with what seemed to be perfection.

"Uncle Ulric is coming back," Georgina said with a different note in her voice than the way she had spoken of him before. "Do you think he will race with us as he did last week?"

"I think he will be very busy," Lara replied, "as the Prince of Wales is coming to stay. So you must not be disappointed if we just have to race on our own."

"It is more fun when Uncle Ulric is there because then there are three horses instead of two," Georgina said with unanswerable logic.

"Let us hope he will remember that you want to see him," Lara said.

The child gave a little sigh, and it struck Lara that it was heartless of the Marquis not to realise what an monotonous existence his niece led despite the fact that she was surrounded by luxury.

'That is another thing about which I shall speak to him,' she promised herself, then laughed at her own presumption.

How could she tell the Marquis of all people what he should or should not do?

And yet she knew that for Georgina's sake she had to try to convince him about her music, and of course it would be better than anything else if other children of her age were frequently invited to the Priory.

"There must be other girls and boys of Georgina's age in the neighbourhood," she said to Nanny.

"If there are, how are we to meet them?" Nanny asked sharply. "You must be aware, Miss Wade, as there's no Lady of the House, family life's something which doesn't count here."

Lara knew that was true. When her mother was alive, it had been she who had invited children to tea, and somehow arranged that Lara was invited back, although they lived in a very isolated part of Essex.

But here, she was sure, things were different: it was not merely a question of the local families being aware of Georgina's existence for them to invite her to their houses, but it was obvious that to start the ball rolling they must first be invited to the Priory.

Lara could see the solution, but the difficulty was how to put her plan into operation, and it all hinged on the Marquis.

She thought it was unlikely that she and Georgina would even see him this week-end.

They finished tea in the School-Room and Georgina was asking somewhat plaintively whether they would be able to go to the Music-Room if there was a party in the house, when the door opened.

Lara looked up expectantly, hoping that by some unexpected piece of good luck it was the Marquis, although that was unlikely, when she saw a familiar red face and Lord Magor came into the room.

Slowly she rose to her feet and as Georgina rose too he said in his plummy voice:

"Hello, little lady, it is nice to see you again. What have you been doing while your uncle and I have been in London?"

He did not wait for an answer but looked at Lara and said with what she thought was an unpleasant smile:

"I hope you are ready to welcome me back, Miss Wade?"

Lara seated herself at the table again.

"We are just having tea, My Lord."

"I guessed that was what you would be doing," Lord Magor said, "and while I am here I will accept a cup from your pretty hands."

He was flirting with her in a manner which Lara

thought was exactly as if he were on stage, and it flashed through her mind once again that she must remember to put it down word for word in her notes.

"I will ring for another cup, My Lord," she said demurely.

"Do not bother, do not bother!" Lord Magor replied. "I really wanted to talk to you."

His eyes flickering over her face seemed to her to be deliberately appraising the colour of her hair, the whiteness of her skin.

Then as he looked at her figure she had the feeling that he was mentally undressing her, and she hated him.

"I am afraid, My Lord," she said, "we cannot ask you to stay as I have a book which I have promised to read to Georgina before she goes to bed. As it is a lesson, you will understand we cannot be disturbed."

Lord Magor laughed.

"Are you trying to get rid of me? Let me tell you, my strict disciplinarian, that if you are determined, so am I. I have come here to see you and my adopted niece, and I have no intention of leaving until I am ready to do so."

He had declared war and Lara knew it.

"Of course, My Lord," she answered, "and if you want to talk to Georgina, I quite understand."

She rose as she spoke and walked across the room to her bedroom door.

"Where are you going, Miss Wade?" Georgina asked nervously. "You said you were going to read to me."

This was something she much enjoyed, for Lara had found several books in the Library containing stories which the child was just old enough to understand, and to which she listened with interest.

"I shall only be in my bedroom," Lara replied, "and if you want me, you have only to call."

"I want you now! Now, at this moment!" Georgina exclaimed.

She rose from the table as she spoke and, avoiding the hand Lord Magor put out to stop her, ran to Lara to hold on to her.

"Read to me, read to me now!" she insisted.

Lara looked over the child's head at Lord Magor.

"I am sorry, My Lord," she said, "but I am sure you understand that my pupil's interests must come first."

Lord Magor rose to his feet with an expression in his eyes which told her he had not enjoyed this small skirmish in which he had been defeated.

"Very well, Miss Wade. You win—for the moment!"

He walked towards the door.

"Good-night Georgina," he said. "I shall tell your uncle you were too ill to talk to me, and I hope that he will not feel you are not well enough to ride tomorrow."

It was a threat which made Lara's temper rise as the School-Room door closed behind him.

"What did he mean...what is he...saying?" Georgina asked. "I am not ill! You know I am not ill, Miss Wade!"

"Of course you are not," Lara said soothingly. "Lord Magor was being disagreeable because you did not wish to talk to him."

"Perhaps, if he tells Uncle Ulric I am ill, I shall not be allowed to ride *Snowball* with you."

"Leave that to me," Lara said. "I promise you we will both ride tomorrow morning, and Lord Magor will not be able to interfere."

She picked up the book they were reading as she spoke, and walked towards the sofa.

"Come and sit down," she said.

Then, as she saw the child was really upset, she said:

"I have a better idea. Let us go to the Music-Room and try out that new Sonata you were playing so well this morning."

Georgina's eyes lit up with excitement.

"Can we do that?"

"Why not?" Lara asked. "But let us hurry in case anyone stops us."

She had a feeling as she and Georgina slipped down a side staircase and along to the Music-Room that she was scoring off Lord Magor and putting him into his proper perspective.

He had tried to hit at her through the child but she knew that once Georgina was immersed in her music she would not worry about riding and Lord Magor would be forgotten.

Because she was still angry, Lara told herself that Jane was right.

He was definitely the villain and a very unpleasant one at that.

chapter five

LARA and Georgina went down the secondary staircase and reached the corridor which led to the Music-
Room.

There appeared to be no one about and they were
just walking quickly along it, when through a door
which led into a room Lara had not seen there came
the Marquis.

She started because it was such a surprise and Georgina looked apprehensively at her uncle.

"Hello, Georgina!" he exclaimed. "Where are you
off to?"

As the Marquis spoke it struck Lara that this was
the opportunity she had been waiting for to tell him
about Georgina.

"Good-evening, Miss Wade."

He spoke dryly, in the manner that was so char-
acteristic of him.

Lara curtsied.

"Good-evening, My Lord, and unless you are very busy, I would like to have a word with you."

The Marquis raised his eyebrows before he replied:

"I am certainly free at this moment, Miss Wade."

Lara turned to Georgina.

"Go to the Music-Room, dear," she said, "and get everything ready. I will join you in a minute or two."

The child was looking nervously at her uncle, afraid that something unusual was happening, but she ran off obediently, her blue sash bobbing up and down on her expensive muslin gown.

Lara looked at the Marquis.

"Well, Miss Wade?" he asked. "Are you prepared to tell me here what is wrong, or would you rather we sat down?"

"It is nothing wrong, My Lord, but perhaps it would be better if we went into a Sitting-Room."

The Marquis turned back towards the room he had just left and opened the door, saying:

"This is where we will not be disturbed."

Lara saw that the room she entered was an office, and by the maps framed and hung on the walls she guessed it was where the Marquis did all his work connected with the Estate.

There was an upright chair on one side of the desk, and as she walked towards it the Marquis seated himself opposite her.

There was a little pause, as if he were feeling for words, and leaning back comfortably in his chair very much at his ease, he said after a moment:

"I am waiting."

She thought he spoke as if he was slightly amused and had already decided that whatever she had to say to him was unimportant and unnecessary.

Instinctively her chin went up and she said:

"I wished to speak to you, My Lord, about Georgina."

She had a feeling it was not what he expected, and he replied:

"If you are going to tell me she is backward, I have already heard that from her other Governesses, and there is obviously nothing I can do about it."

"On the contrary," Lara said quickly, "what I am going to tell you may come as a surprise, but in my opinion Georgina could undoubtedly be a very talented, if not an exceptional, musician."

The Marquis looked as if he could not believe what she had said:

"How do you know?" he asked.

"You may not think I am qualified to judge," Lara replied, "but I have been taught to play the piano and I am certain in my own mind that if Georgina had the right teachers she could be almost, if not quite, up to professional standard."

"How can you possibly know this?" the Marquis enquired, "after being here only a week?"

Lara smiled.

"What I am going to suggest, My Lord, is that you hear Georgina play. You must of course remember that she has had no music lessons except those I have given her, and she is at the moment playing entirely by ear, having listened to the pieces I have played for her first."

She paused before she added emphatically:

"I shall be very surprised if you do not find what she can already do extraordinary."

The Marquis was silent. Then he said:

"I admit I am astonished at what you have just told me, Miss Wade, and I was also surprised to find that

103

Georgina can ride so well. Every other Governess she had, with the exception of Miss Cooper who I think was too frightened to speak to me, has complained of the child's lethargy and indifference to every subject, and what amounted to almost a determination not to learn."

Lara did not answer for a moment while she considered how she could put into words what she wanted to say. Then she replied:

"Georgina is a very sensitive child, and I think her whole life has been upset by the fact that she knows that both her father and mother resented her being a girl instead of a boy."

"How could she possibly know that?" the Marquis asked sharply.

"Servants always talk in front of children as if they were deaf," Lara replied. "Apparently one of them actually said in her hearing that her mother wept when she was born because she was not the son they wanted. And her father made it very clear to Georgina that he was disappointed that she was not a boy."

The Marquis did not speak and Lara said:

"An added blow of Fate which has wounded the child is that she now realises also that if she had been a boy she would now be in your place."

She had now again startled the Marquis, who stared at her as if he could not believe what he was hearing.

"Did she say that to you?" he asked. "Or did you put the idea into her head?"

Lara stiffened and the Marquis saw the anger in her eyes. Then before she could speak he said quickly:

"I apologise. I should not have said that."

"I accept your apology, My Lord, but I am humiliated that you should think even for a moment, I would do such a thing."

"Forgive me," the Marquis said. "I can only plead as an excuse that I know very little about children."

"Then may I just say one thing more, My Lord?" Lara said, "as we are talking frankly?"

"As *you* are talking frankly, Miss Wade," the Marquis interposed.

"Very well," Lara replied, "and if you are angry I may as well get it all over at once."

"I will try not to be too incensed," he said, "even though I think you are insinuating that I have been extremely stupid where my niece is concerned."

"I am not prepared to be as rude as that, My Lord," Lara answered, "but shall we say you have not given her the same attention or shown her the same interest that you give to your horses?"

The Marquis laughed somewhat ruefully before he said:

"Very well, I accept your condemnation. Now tell me, what is on your mind?"

"I cannot help thinking that as she is an orphan and therefore a lonely, introspective child who feels she is unwanted, the best thing possible would be for her to entertain other children and if possible have them here to do lessons with her."

Lara drew in her breath before she went on quickly:

"At the moment she spends her time only with grown-ups and Nanny is not only very possessive but also treats her as if she were a baby."

As she finished Lara half-expected the Marquis to snap back at her and tell her she was being impertinent in criticising both him and his household.

Instead he said slowly:

"I think I understand what you are saying, Miss

Wade. Will you allow me to think it over and to give, as you suggest, the same attention to my niece that I give my horses?"

Lara gave him a smile that seemed to light her whole face.

"That is all I am asking, My Lord. Thank you very much."

She rose to her feet as she spoke and added:

"And now, please, will you come and hear Georgina play?"

"That is what I intend to do," the Marquis said, "and I hope you will not be too disappointed or indeed too angry with me if I do not agree with your opinion that she will make a good musician."

He walked towards the door and opened it for Lara. As he joined her outside and they walked down the corridor towards the Music-Room, he said:

"As if happens, I am considered to be quite an authority on music, being a Director of Covent Garden, and the Prince of Wales frequently asks me to choose the artistes who shall entertain his guests at Marlborough House."

"Then you are obviously just the right person to help Georgina."

"That remains to be seen," the Marquis said, as if he was trying to prevent himself from being carried away by her enthusiasm.

They walked in silence to the Music-Room. Then as they neared the door Lara held up her hand and the Marquis stopped.

They could hear Georgina playing, and Lara knew that nobody could pretend that it was the ordinary sound to be expected from a child of her age.

Instead the melody of the Strauss Waltz which came flowing out towards them had a depth of rhythm and was played with such feeling that it might easily have come from the fingers of an acknowledged concert pianist.

After two or three seconds Lara, without speaking, opened the door and went into the room.

Georgina, looking very small on the dais beside the huge Broadwood, was so intent on what she was doing that she did not even notice they were there.

Then as she finished with an octave her small fingers could only just reach, she looked up and her hands fell into her lap.

"That was very good, Georgina!" Lara said. "Now I want you to play for your uncle the piece you played for me yesterday."

"Perhaps...Uncle Ulric does not...like my being...here," Georgina said nervously.

"I am delighted the Music-Room is being used for a change," the Marquis contradicted. "I think it must have felt neglected for quite a long time."

"I may go on playing here?" Georgina asked.

She spoke as if the idea that she might be turned away and isolated from the piano had been worrying her, and the Marquis answered:

"I suggest you play something else, and I will then tell you if I appreciate your playing as much as Miss Wade does."

"Miss Wade thinks I could be very good if I tried hard."

"So she has been telling me," the Marquis said, "and now you can tell me far more eloquently by playing than by words."

Georgina smiled as if the idea amused her. Then she said:

"Yes, of course, Uncle Ulric."

She started to play an aria from the opera *La Tra-*

viata, which Lara had played to her at the beginning of the week and which had caught her fancy.

It was quite a strenuous composition and not, Lara thought, the soft dreamy sort of music the Marquis would have expected from a child.

Because she thought it was a mistake to encroach too closely on Georgina, she deliberately sat down on the sofa a little way from the piano.

As if he understood, the Marquis also moved away to lean against one of the pillars.

First of all he watched Georgina, then Lara was aware, even though she did not look at him, that he was watching her.

It made her feel shy.

At the same time she was so anxious for Georgina to succeed in impressing her uncle that she could not relax, but sat upright, her fingers laced together in her lap, and although she was almost unaware of it, she was praying.

As always when she was at the piano, Georgina after a short hesitation became completely absorbed in the music and oblivious of everything else.

She was swept away into a world of her own which was different from anything she had known before in her dull little life.

When she finished there was an unmistakable radiance in her face.

Just for a moment, as she took her hands from the keys, she did not move, and Lara knew she was still in her dream-world before she came back to the reality of where she was and what was happening.

She did not speak, but sat waiting until with a little sigh that seemed to come from the very depths of her body she asked:

"Was that . . . all right?"

She looked at Lara, who said:

"It was very good considering you have only played it two or three times before."

As she spoke she looked at the Marquis challengingly as if she dared him to disagree.

He walked towards the piano.

"As Miss Wade has said, that was very good, Georgina," he said, "and now we have to decide what we shall do about you in the future."

"What do you . . . mean?"

"If you are going to be a musician," he replied, "you will have to have the very best teachers and it may be possible to find somebody here in the country who could teach you for a year or so. But I think ultimately it will mean you will have to be in London at least during the week to study with somebody from the Royal Academy of Music."

"That sounds very exciting, Uncle Ulric!" Georgina said. "But will I also be able to ride in London?"

"I thought that question would arise sooner or later," the Marquis smiled, "and the answer is of course yes. It will mean riding in the Park, as I do every morning, but you will still be able to gallop on the race-course when you come home on Saturdays and Sundays."

Georgina looked up at him.

"It sounds wonderful! Wonderful, Uncle Ulric! Do you really mean I can do that, and learn to play as well as Miss Wade thinks I will be able to?"

"I have a feeling you will have to work very hard to live up to her expectations," the Marquis replied.

He looked at Lara as he spoke and she had the feeling he was being slightly provocative.

Then he said, as if he wished to be honest:

"You are of course quite right, Miss Wade, and

before you say it for me, this is something I should have found out a long time ago."

Lara gave a little laugh.

"You are being unexpectedly generous, My Lord, but I have always been told to beware of 'the Greeks when they come bearing gifts!'"

The Marquis's eyes twinkled and it seemed to erase for the moment the cynical lines on his face.

"Now that you and your protegée have convinced me of what has to be done," he said, "I shall certainly concentrate on it and give it priority over the other items demanding my attention."

"Thank you, My Lord," Lara said with delight. "I cannot tell you how happy this makes me."

Almost as if she could read the Marquis's thoughts she knew that he was wondering why the child whom she had met only a week ago mattered so much to her, but thought it a mistake to ask the question, which she suspected trembled on his lips, in front of Georgina.

She knew it would have been impossible to tell him the truth, but although she had never been unwanted, she had known the loneliness of being a child without other children to play with.

Also in a small way she had felt she had a talent that she should express, although she was not quite certain how she could do so.

It flashed through her mind that all this could form part of her novel, but until this moment she had not concerned herself with the children in it who were just shadowy figures to whom she had given no substance.

"Shall I play you something else, Uncle Ulric?" Georgina asked eagerly. "Miss Wade has taught me a very gay Waltz by Offenbach which she said she is sure you dance to when you go to Balls in London."

The Marquis flashed a quizzical glance at Lara, but he merely answered:

"I should enjoy hearing you play it, Georgina."

Georgina struck the first chord, then she was playing one of the tunes which had captured the imagination of Paris and which to Lara typified all the gaiety of the Balls she had read about and imagined, but had never attended.

Because Georgina played well, the music made Lara want to dance, and in her imagination she was gliding around the room in a dazzlingly beautiful gown in the arms of a handsome partner.

Then as the melody came to an end she realised that once again the Marquis was looking at her and, she thought, questioningly.

'Perhaps he thinks I should not have talked about him in such a way to Georgina,' she thought uncomfortably.

Because the idea perturbed her, she rose to her feet.

"That was very good," the Marquis approved. "In fact let me say once and for all, Georgina, I am very impressed with how you play the piano, and I promise you shall play as often and as much as you like with the best teachers I can provide."

"Thank you—thank you, Uncle Ulric," Georgina cried, "and perhaps if I try very hard, one day you will be...proud of me."

Lara drew in her breath, wondering if the Marquis would understand how much his answer to this remark meant to Georgina. It was as if for the moment she had transferred her longing for the father and mother she no longer had, to him.

She also felt that if he failed the child now she would never forgive him.

"I am very proud of you already, Georgina," he said in his deep voice, "just as I was proud when you won our race. I think we ought to have another tomorrow morning. Do you agree?"

He put out his hand as he spoke and Georgina slipped hers into it.

"That would be lovely, Uncle Ulric, and if *Snowball* beats *Black Knight* again I am sure he will become very conceited."

"I am sure he will," the Marquis replied, "so perhaps I had better not give him such a big start as he had last time."

"But, please—very nearly as long," Georgina pleaded.

The Marquis smiled.

"We will have to see tomorrow morning, and of course it all depends on how well you ride him."

"I know that," Georgina said, "and I am trying to ride as well as you and Miss Wade do."

"You are quite right to do that," the Marquis said, "as we are both rather exceptional."

Holding Georgina by the hand he stepped down with her from the dais on which the piano stood and came towards Lara.

The Marquis's understanding and kindness to Georgina made her feel so happy that she looked at him and said very softly, feeling he would understand:

"Thank you . . . My Lord."

* * *

Nanny put Georgina to bed, having been rather disagreeable because they were late in coming upstairs and also because the child was excited at what had happened. She was obviously jealous and Lara went to her own room to change before she had supper.

Because her mother had always insisted that they change for dinner at home, however meagre the meal might be, she always had a bath at seven o'clock and, even though she ate alone at the Priory, changed into a different gown from the one she had worn all day.

She had little choice of what she could wear, seeing that her own wardrobe was so scanty and Jane's clothes were not much better.

There was one rather pretty blue semi-evening gown which Lara had not yet tried and was rather anxious to do so.

Then she told herself it was a waste of time, and it was also wrong to wear out Jane's precious clothes when it was unlikely that, like herself, she would be able to afford more than one or two really useful frocks every year.

She was taking one of her own gowns from the wardrobe when Agnes came into the room.

"Sorry I'm late, Miss," she said, "but we've been ever so busy downstairs."

"Why is that?" Lara enquired. "I thought the house-party was arriving tomorrow."

"That's what we all thought," Agnes replied, "but when His Lordship got back he said fifteen people were arriving late this evening instead of tomorrow as we expected, so as to be here before the Prince of Wales and Lady Brooke."

"Oh, I see!" Lara exclaimed. "So I suppose you have been unpacking for those who have just arrived."

"It's been a real rush to get it all down before dinner," Agnes complained, "and the visitors' own lady's-maids, because they've had long journeys, only want to supervise and leave us to do all the hard word."

"All the same, it cannot be hard work to unpack all those pretty clothes you have been describing to me."

"I tell you what we'll do, Miss," Agnes said, as if she had just thought of it. "Tomorrow night when I'm tidying the bedrooms, which I usually have to do when the rest of the staff have gone down to supper, I'll take you with me and show you some of the lovely gowns that Lady Lesley has brought with her."

"Has Lady Louise come again?" Lara asked curiously.

"Yes, and from all I hears His Lordship wasn't expecting her. She just turned up with Lord Magor and says she was intending to stay with somebody else, but they've let her down and she was sure His Lordship'd be pleased to see her."

"How do you know she said that?" Lara enquired.

"Mr. Newman, the Butler, was telling us what Her Ladyship said when he announced her and Lord Magor. But he also says he fancied His Lordship was none too pleased to see her! That did not surprise all of us, for there's been bets in the Servants' Hall as to how soon His Lordship'd be looking for a new face."

Lara suddenly felt ashamed, not of Agnes but of herself.

It was one thing to want copy for her book, but another, she felt, to discuss the Marquis with his servants.

She did not know why she suddenly felt ashamed, she only knew she wished she had never asked Agnes any questions or had ever heard of Lady Louise.

"Will you do up my dress, Agnes?" she asked, changing the subject. "Otherwise I will be late for my supper when it comes upstairs and I hate food which is cold."

"Yes, of course, Miss, and tomorrow night I'll take you down with me when they're all safe and sound in the Housekeeper's room."

Lara did not answer and she told herself when Agnes had left that she would not do anything so reprehensible as to inspect anyone's gowns when they were not aware of it.

At the same time she could not help thinking of what inestimable value all this was for her novel.

This past week she had written the whole of the third chapter, and she was sure her description of the heroine's feelings at seeing the Duke's ancestral home—which was of course based on the Priory—was better than anything she had ever written before.

'I know I am going to sell this book, and make money both for Papa and me,' she thought, 'and if I have to do things of which Mama would not approve, I must not be too squeamish about it.'

At the same time she was determined that however adventurous she might be she would not go into Lady Louise's room.

"I am sorry for her," she told herself, "sorry that she has been made unhappy by losing the Marquis, but of course it is very wrong for her to be interested in him in the first place when she is married."

Then she thought it would be impossible for her to describe what a married woman felt for a man she could not marry and how she justified herself in being unfaithful to her husband.

'I must keep to a straight, happy love-story,' she thought.

Then she was well aware now that she had learnt as much as she had already about the Marquis's friends and the behaviour of the Prince of Wales, that her story would certainly not sound authentic if the love affairs in it were all pure, innocent, and completely blameless.

'Perhaps the only way I can make money,' she thought, 'is just by being a Governess.'

She wondered if that was what she would do when she left the Priory.

Then it struck her that when she did leave she was going to miss not only Georgina, but the Marquis's horses and indeed the Marquis himself.

Although she found him over-powering, she knew it was a fascination she had never expected to talk to him because he was so different from any man she had ever met before.

Not only was he a magnificent rider, but he had, she was aware, an extremely intelligent mind.

Although Jane had not mentioned it, Lara had realised since she had been at the Priory that the efficiency with which it was run, the excellence of the servants, and the prosperity of the estate were all due to the direction which came from the top: in other words from the owner.

Her father had once said that what people needed were inspiration, guidance, and an ideal to aim for, and she knew that in his own way that was what the Marquis gave those who served him.

The servants, one after another, were always saying in their own words:

"This's what His Lordship expects." "His Lordship'll be angry if we don't do this." "We expect things to be perfect at the Priory!"

That was what made the whole place, Lara was

certain, an example that perhaps other, similar, houses tried to emulate but not so successfully.

Inevitably the question she found herself asking was why, when he had so much, did the Marquis look bored, cynical and, as she was sure in her own mind, unhappy?

She wished she were brave enough to ask him what was wrong, then laughed at the idea of being so inquisitive.

She finished her supper, the footman took away the tray and, as she knew that nobody else would return that evening, she locked the door of the School-Room.

Tonight, because she wished to write down in full what had happened when the Marquis listened to Georgina playing the piano, she got out her manuscript books and first of all made notes which she realised had become, since she had been at the Priory, more and more like a Diary.

When her notes were completed she started Chapter Four.

She realised that so far what she had written had been entirely about the heroine.

Now it was time to introduce the hero and she began to describe the Duke, only to realise after she had written nearly two pages that she had in fact described very accurately and rather cleverly the Marquis himself.

She reread what she had written and asked:

'Do I really intend him to be the hero?'

He would certainly fit the Ducal coronet without any difficulty. At the same time, the dream-man she had envisaged before she came to the Priory had been very different.

She was not certain what an innocent, wide-eyed

Governess who was like Jane would feel about a man who was like the Marquis.

'She would be afraid of him,' Lara thought.

Once again she looked back over what she had written and as she did so she heard a slight sound and, looking across the room, saw the handle of the door turn.

Thinking for a moment that she must have imagined it, she watched the handle turn again and was aware that somebody was outside, and knew who it was.

There was a knock on the door, soft enough to be made by a person who did not wish to be overheard.

Lara did not move, but she knew whoever was outside would have seen the light under the door and known that she was not in her bedroom.

Then she heard a voice, little above a whisper but quite clear, say:

"Miss Wade, I want to speak to you!"

Now there was no doubt who was there and for a moment Lara felt her heart leap in fear.

Then she remembered the strong lock on the door and sat back in her chair careful to make no noise, enjoying the feeling that Lord Magor was locked out and there was nothing he could do about it.

She heard his voice again.

"I must speak to you. Let me in."

She knew he was listening to hear her response.

Then after several seconds, as if he realised he was defeated, she heard him move away and go slowly and carefully down the stairs.

It was then she clasped her hands together with delight and wanted to jump up and dance because he had been made to look a fool.

'That should teach him to leave wretched Governesses alone,' she thought, and wondered how he had escaped so early from the party downstairs.

Then she looked at the clock on the mantelpiece and realised to her surprise, for she had no idea how long she had been writing, that it was after one o'clock. She suspected that the first night after their journey the party had gone to bed early.

She realised how frightened Jane would have been in her place and she thought it was entirely her own fault.

'I suppose she thought the servants would think it queer if she locked the door,' Lara ruminated.

Personally she did not care what they thought, although she had every intention, if she woke in time, of unlocking the door before the house-maids came to clean the School-Room.

"How dare Lord Magor behave in such a disgraceful way?" she asked aloud.

She knew if she had let him in he would have tried to make love to her, whatever that entailed, and perhaps if she allowed him to do so, he would have stayed with her for hours.

She suddenly remembered something which had escaped her mind until now.

The first morning she had been at the Priory she had been woken by a loud bell ringing at six o'clock.

For a moment it had flashed through her mind that it might be a fire-alarm, but when no commotion had followed she had known there must be another reason for it.

When Agnes had called her later that morning she had asked:

"What was the bell I heard which woke me up so early?"

"That's the stable-yard bell, Miss," Agnes explained. "It's always rung at six o'clock when there are guests in the house. We never used to have it, but I understand when His Lordship was staying at Easton Lodge, where the Prince of Wales stays so often, Lady Brooke had the stable-yard bell always rung at six and he thought it would be a good idea."

Lara had not thought of it again, but now it came to her mind that the reason for the bell was to warn those who had to return to their own bedrooms before the house-maids were moving about.

'How can that be the explanation?' she argued, but some instinct told her it was.

'The whole thing is disgraceful,' she thought, 'and Papa would certainly be shocked at my staying in a house where immorality is encouraged in such a blatant way.'

She only hoped her father would never learn of the things that were coming to her notice at the Priory.

Then she thought perhaps he knew a great deal more about London Society than she did. After all, no one had been more raffish or more extravagant than her grandfather.

She had often been told, although it had not had any significance for her when she was young, that her Uncle Edward, who should have come into the title, was a great Dasher, not only on the battle-field but in the Ball-Room.

She had not understood what was meant by such a statement, but now she remembered that her father had said that his elder brother had never married because he found it difficult to find one woman who would satisfy him for the rest of his life.

"He certainly pursued a considerable number in his search," he had said to his wife within Lara's hearing, "but he was not so fortunate as I was, my darling, in finding you."

"I am very grateful," Lady Hurlington had said softly, "although I have often been jealous of the women who hang breathlessly on your every word, and are all too eager to help you in Church."

Lara's father had laughed.

"They all look to me a hundred and one!" he had answered, "and even if they were as beautiful as the Venus de Milo, I assure you, my darling, I would not even notice them when you are there."

'That is what being in love is like,' Lara told herself now, and it was what she had meant to describe in her book and thought at first it would be easy.

Now it seemed there were many sorts of love, including the love that Lady Louise had for the Marquis which was wrong and wicked, and yet she could still remember the heart-break which had echoed in her voice.

There was the love of the Prince of Wales for Lady Brooke, who was years younger than he was and had a good-looking and charming husband who was always being referred to in the newspapers and magazines as if he was a pillar of the aristocratic world.

"Why can she not be content with him, even though it must be very exciting to have the Prince of Wales as her lover?" Lara asked.

It all seemed rather incomprehensible, and yet now when she had the opportunity to find out a great deal more about these people, she knew her father would definitely disapprove.

But he would perhaps forgive her when her book was a success. They would be able to do up the Vicarage, live much more comfortably than they did at the moment.

Yet Lara knew she was making excuses for something which both repelled and yet fascinated her.

She thought of Lord Magor and knew that somehow she had to make certain that when she left he would not pursue Jane any more.

She was so easily frightened and in a way so helpless that Lara thought she would have been scared into hysterics if she had been in her place this evening.

She remembered Jane had said that she lay awake all night, unable to sleep because even with her bedroom door locked she was afraid Lord Magor would somehow get at her.

"His behaviour is appalling!" Lara told herself. "If I cannot manage to scare him off in any other way, I will tell the Marquis."

After the Marquis had been so helpful and understanding over Georgina, she thought perhaps he would be just as sympathetic about Lord Magor.

At the same time he was his friend, and to condemn him for behaving badly in running after a young woman, or rather women, would be also to condemn the Marquis for breaking the hearts of Alice, Gladys, Charlotte, and Lady Louise.

Actually the boot was on the other foot as they were pursuing him.

At the same time Lara realised he must have made love to them in the first place, otherwise they would not have lost their hearts.

Everything she thought about made her plan of writing a novel about this type of society become more and more complicated.

"Perhaps my heroine should just fall in love with the boy next door who would be the Squire's son," she told herself, "and they will live happily ever afterwards."

But she knew she was not going to be able to write a long and complicated plot around the village of Little Fladbury, and if there were no obstacles and no difficulties, it would soon become boring after two or three thousand words.

'No, it has got to be the Duke,' she decided, 'and like the Prince of Wales, he will undoubtedly make love to all the lovely ladies who are married to somebody else.'

Because it seemed almost ridiculous, she found herself laughing.

Then she put away her manuscript book, turned out the light, and going into her bedroom, locked the door securely before she started to undress and get into bed.

chapter six

THE next day Georgina was disappointed when they reached the race-course and there was no sign of the Marquis.

"I thought Uncle Ulric was going to race us," she said plaintively.

"Never mind," Lara answered. "We will practise racing together, then when he does come perhaps we shall both beat him."

This appealed to Georgina and Lara gave her a long start, then managed to pull *Glorious* in to let her win by nearly a length.

"Uncle Ulric would think that good!" Georgina said excitedly.

"Of course he would," Lara agreed.

They had two long races and a shorter one, and then as Lara thought the child had had enough they started riding back through the woods.

The sun was coming through the branches and it was so lovely that she felt her mind slipping away into a romantic dream, so that she started when Georgina gave a cry and exclaimed:

"There is Uncle Ulric, and he is coming to find us."

It was indeed the Marquis and he was riding *Black Knight* towards them. Perhaps it was because Georgina sounded excited that Lara felt her heart leap too.

The Marquis was certainly looking magnificent, almost, she thought, like a Knight in ancient days going out to kill a dragon, and she drew *Glorious* to a stand-still letting Georgina ride towards her uncle, exclaiming as she went:

"You are late, Uncle Ulric, too late to race us, but I beat Miss Wade—twice!"

"I am very sorry I was delayed," the Marquis said, "and I hope you will forgive me."

He was speaking to Georgina but he was looking at Lara, and as she smiled in response he said:

"I had not forgotten my engagement with you both, and tomorrow I will definitely try to be more punctual."

"Tomorrow is Sunday," Lara pointed out, "and that means, My Lord, we shall have to ride either before Church or afterwards."

The Marquis's eyes twinkled.

"I can see, Miss Wade, you are definitely pointing out to me the path of righteousness."

"What you do, My Lord, is of course not my concern," Lara replied, "but I think Georgina should go to Church."

"Yes, indeed," he answered.

She thought he spoke a little cynically and there was a twist to his lips as if he thought she was definitely censuring the type of household that did not treat the Sabbath as a Holy Day.

"Why do you not come to Church with us, Uncle Ulric?" Georgina asked. "Papa used to read the lessons, and he made them sound much more exciting than when the Parson read them."

"That is an invitation I shall have to consider," the Marquis answered.

Again his eyes met Lara's and there was an expression in them, she thought, which dared her to criticise him.

"I shall not offer to race you now," he said, "as I expect your horses have had enough for one day, but I suggest we ride through the Park together. The Head-Keeper has just informed me that there is a fox's lair in the wood on the other side, and perhaps you would like to see the baby foxes before they are killed."

"Killed?" Georgina cried in consternation. "Why must they be killed?"

"Because if we leave them they will kill a lot of pheasants and also the chickens on the farm, which will mean you will have no eggs for your breakfast," the Marquis replied.

Georgina considered this for some time, then she asked:

"Will the baby cubs really do so much damage?"

"I am afraid so," he answered. "But forget for the moment what lies ahead of them, and just think they look young, which is something which unfortunately for all of us does not last long."

The way he spoke made Lara laugh.

"Why are you laughing, Miss Wade?" he enquired.

"Because you sound, My Lord, as if you are Methuselah."

"That is how I feel at the moment," the Marquis replied.

He made no explanation as to why he was feeling like that, and rode on in silence.

They saw the baby cubs which were only small balls of fluff, and as Lara could see no sign of the mother she assumed that the vixen had already been killed.

Then she and Georgina rode home alone as the Marquis said he had to visit one of the farms.

"I do not want the baby foxes to be killed," Georgina said.

"Neither do I," Lara agreed, "but when we do lessons on Nature Study you will learn that the animals prey on each other and foxes will kill not only the pheasants and chickens, but also the rabbits which you love and anything else they can catch, not only for food but because they enjoy killing."

Georgina thought this over and she said:

"It is very, very wicked to be cruel to something small and helpless, is it not, Miss Wade?"

"Yes, it is," Lara said firmly and she was thinking of Lord Magor.

After last night she realised exactly why Jane was so frightened of him, and she wondered how many other pathetic, lonely Governesses had shrunk away from him in fear, and yet been unable to prevent him from making their lives a misery.

'I hate him!' she thought. 'He is a bully and a tryant, and sooner or later I will get even with him!'

She thought perhaps he would come back to the School-Room at tea-time, but there was no sign of him and she learnt not only from the servants but from all the commotion that was taking place downstairs that by now the Prince of Wales, Lady Brooke, and all the Marquis's other guests had arrived.

Despite her resolution, when Nanny was putting Georgina to bed and Agnes put her head in through the door of the bedroom, Lara was waiting expectantly.

"Come quickly, Miss!" she said, "and you'll see the ladies going down to dinner."

Lara did not answer. She merely followed Agnes up another staircase, to the top floor, and they went along a narrow passage until they reached the centre of the house.

Here as Lara looked down she could see three floors with the Grand Staircase rising upwards from each one.

"Nobody looks up as high as this," Agnes said, "and if you leans over the bannister Miss, no one'll notice you."

They were joined a moment later by four of the younger house-maids who looked a little shy at seeing Lara, but were reassured when she smiled at them.

Looking right down into the Hall Lara could see the footmen in their smart evening-livery, wearing powdered wigs and white silk stockings with satin breeches.

Then just before eight o'clock the first lady appeared on the stairs.

She wore so many diamonds on her head, around her neck, and on her wrists that she seemed to be enveloped with a light which came from herself.

At this angle her gown certainly seemed very décolleté, at the same time very elaborate and exquisitely beautiful.

She was followed almost immediately by several

other ladies, two of them accompanied by gentlemen in black knee-breeches, one of whom was wearing the blue Order of the Garter across his chest.

One after another the house-party descended the stairway like wave upon wave of glittering beauty that made Lara speechless.

They moved like graceful swans gliding over a lake and their voices and laughter seemed to drift up towards the on-lookers almost as if it was a mist rising over the stream in the Park.

When so many had passed down that Lara had ceased to count them there was a little pause.

Then she saw a dazzling figure in a white gown embroidered all over with diamanté, her fair hair almost obscured by a huge tiara, and knew who it was even before Agnes whispered:

"Lady Brooke!"

Accompanying her was the already somewhat burly figure of the Prince of Wales.

They walked down side by side, and although they did not touch each other there was something in the way Lady Brooke lifted her face up to his and he looked down at her which revealed their feelings without words.

"It is wrong!" Lara tried to say.

At the same time it struck her that love, wherever one found it, could be very wonderful.

Then the Prince and Lady Brooke passed together across the marble Hall and Lara knew they had joined the other members of the house-party in the Silver Salon.

She gave a little sigh.

"Now you see how lovely she is," Agnes said. "That gown must be worth a fortune!"

Lara did not answer.

She was thinking how she could describe in words what she had just seen and how it was important she should get it down on paper while it was still fresh in her mind.

She walked back with Agnes to the staircase which led down to the School-Room floor, and the house-maid said:

"I've got to go now, Miss, but I'll come back for you as soon as the lady's-maids have all gone to supper, but that won't be for a couple of hours."

Lara had already learnt that in all big houses the senior servants ate in the Housekeeper's room and that included the visiting lady's-maids and valets.

The meal in the Servants'-Hall began when dinner in the Dining-Room had finished, and so Agnes was right in saying she would not fetch her for at least two hours.

She knew she could occupy herself during that time in writing and she settled down at the School-Room table, first of all making notes, then making her heroine watch, just as she had done, the Duke's house-party going down to dinner.

'She will long to be with them,' Lara told herself, 'she will feel lonely and neglected and jealous because he would not be thinking of her, but of the lovely bejewelled ladies who would be fawning on him because of his high rank as a nobleman.'

Then she thought there might be other reasons as well.

Lady Louise loved the Marquis for himself as a man, for since she was in fact the daughter of a Duke, as Lara had learned, she was not impressed by his title or his possessions.

'He no longer loves her,' Lara thought, 'but she is lucky that he has been interested in her at all.'

131

She found herself wondering what the Marquis would say if he was in love with somebody, and what it would feel like if he kissed the woman he loved.

It was somehow difficult to think of him looking anything but rather bored and cynical, and try as she would she could not make a mental picture of him in the person of the Duke kissing her heroine.

'Perhaps because I have never been kissed it is something I shall never be able to describe,' she thought.

She knew that if Lord Magor kissed her it would be a horror and degradation that she would never wish to write about or remember.

She had sat for a long time not writing, but thinking, when suddenly Agnes reappeared in the doorway:

"Come on, Miss," she said. "They've all gone downstairs now."

It flashed through Lara's mind that this was the moment when she should behave with propriety and stay where she was.

But the temptation was too great and she followed Agnes, who was already hurrying down the stairs to the next floor.

"I'm later, Miss, than I expected," she said when Lara caught up with her, "because Her Ladyship's maid hung about fussing over this and that, and twice I had to remind her she'd be late for supper."

"Would that worry her?" Lara asked.

"Oh no, Miss. She gives herself terrible airs since her lady's always with His Royal Highness. More Royal than the Royals, she is, and we laugh about her behind her back."

Lara laughed too! They had reached the part of the house where she knew the State Bedrooms were all situated, although she had never seen them.

"That's where the Prince is sleeping, Miss," Agnes said pointing to one door, "with a Sitting-Room next to it. Then Lady Brooke's in what's known as the 'Queen's Room.' And her boudoir on the other side of that."

Lara said nothing, but she knew what this arrangement implied.

"His Lordship sleeps in the Master Suite, at the end of the corridor," Agnes went on, pointing to where there was a pair of large doors. "Lady Louise was very annoyed when she found 'her room,' as she calls it, which is next door, had been given to another lady in the party."

Lara said nothing and after a moment Agnes continued:

"I expected them to change the list as she'd come so unexpectedly, but Mrs. Blossom had orders from Mr. Simpson to leave things as they were."

Lara thought she knew why Lady Louise had not been placed next to the Marquis, but then she told herself she did not wish to think about it.

"Show me Lady Brooke's gowns quickly, Agnes," she said, "I am frightened that if I stay long somebody will see me."

"No one's likely to, Miss," Agnes replied. "When there's a house-party, they eats the same as the house guests have in the Dining-Room. Mr. Newman and Mrs. Blossom sees to that. Got to keep up with Easton Lodge and the other houses the Master stays in!"

Lara was sure it was a competition in which if things were not better at the Priory than anywhere else the head-servants would lose face.

Because she did not wish to gossip with Agnes,

but just to see the gowns which she could then describe in detail, she followed her into Lady Brooke's bedroom.

It was a large and very beautiful room which had obviously been renovated and decorated several centuries after the Priory had been built.

The ceiling was painted with a picture of goddesses and cupids, the bed was carved with cupids and doves, and the hangings like the panels let into the white and gold walls were of blue brocade.

The Aubusson carpet and French furniture were, Lara thought, like something out of a dream.

Agnes was already opening a large wardrobe at the far end of the room and Lara could see a kaleidoscope in every colour of the rainbow moving in the breeze from the opening doors almost as if the gowns themselves were alive.

Agnes took them down one by one and Lara could only think that no Queen could have a more magnificent and elaborate trousseau.

There were silks and satins that were as soft as the clouds in the sky, laces embroidered with diamanté which made them appear as if they were covered with dew-drops.

There were chiffons and tulles, ribbons and frills in such profusion that it was difficult after a little while to do anything but think that only a genius could have created such an exquisite frame for a beautiful woman.

"Her Ladyship has jewels to match them all," Agnes said. "She's got diamonds on tonight, and there's a whole set of sapphires, including a tiara, locked away in her jewel-box, besides emeralds, rubies, and turquoises which are ever so lovely with her fair hair."

"I never imagined any woman could have so many clothes all at once!" Lara exclaimed.

Agnes laughed.

"These are only a few of what Her Ladyship owns. Her lady's-maid was telling me she's got two wardrobe rooms at Easton Lodge packed with gowns. Some of them her wears once and never again."

"I suppose that is being really rich," Lara said wistfully.

She was thinking how wonderful it would be just to own one gown like the ones she was looking at.

As she thought of it she wondered whether if she was dressed like Lady Brooke the Marquis would admire her.

Then she almost laughed at the idea that he would even notice her when there were beauties all around him like those she had seen that evening going down to dinner.

"Let me show you Her Ladyship's bonnets," Agnes was saying.

She opened another door of the wardrobe where there were three shelves on which there were bonnets and hats again in every colour, some trimmed with ostrich plumes, others with flowers or ribbons.

They were all in the latest fashion which Lara had seen in the 'Ladies Journal,' but never expected to have actually in front of her.

She longed to put one on and see how she looked in a hat that turned up in front and was trimmed in a way which gave it, she was sure, a *chic* that could only come from Paris.

"I'll show you something, Miss, that'll make you laugh."

Agnes opened a drawer and Lara saw dozens and dozens of gloves laid out neatly so that it was easy to pick up the pair that was wanted.

Some were long white kid to be worn in the evening, some were coloured suede, obviously to match some particular ensemble, others were of leather or lace.

It seemed to Lara incredible that there could be so much variety.

Agnes laughed at her expression.

"It's just the same with shoes," she said. "I think Her Ladyship travels with at least fifty pairs!"

"No wonder she needs a special train to get here!" Lara smiled.

"His Royal Highness has nearly as much luggage as she has, besides two valets, a footman and a brusher, a groom-in-waiting, two equerries, and a secretary who always travel with him."

"I can see he is not a very easy person to entertain," Lara said.

"No indeed, Miss, but everybody's ever so proud and eager to have him as a guest."

"That I can understand."

Once again Lara was looking at the room and wondering what it would be like to sleep in such beautiful surroundings and know that you could buy everything you wanted, and have the most important man in the country in love with you.

She could not help feeling that Lady Brooke was very, very lucky, and yet it was not the perfect happiness which Lara wanted to find in her own life, and to write about in her novel.

How could it be when the Prince and Lady Brooke were each married to other people and, however much they loved each other, there could be no happy ending to their story.

'What I want is to love somebody as Mama loved

Papa,' Lara thought, 'and to feel really and truly in my heart that nothing else was of any importance.'

Agnes was shutting the wardrobe door.

"I'd better get on with my work now, Miss." she said, "otherwise I'll be in trouble."

"Yes, of course," Lara replied, "and thank you very much, Agnes, for all the interesting things you have shown me. I never imagined that anyone could have such beautiful clothes."

"As my mother used to say: 'It costs nothing to look!'"

"No," Lara agreed, "I have enjoyed looking and thank you again."

"That's all right, Miss," Agnes replied.

She started to take the cover off the bed which was of valuable antique lace lined with blue satin.

Lara walked towards the door.

She took one last look around the room, thinking she must imprint it on her mind so that she could describe every detail.

Then she went out into the passage.

She realised as she did so that the suite occupied by Lady Brooke and the Prince was quite a long way from the main staircase in the centre of the house, and she would have to walk from the East Wing to the West Wing before she reached the staircase which led up to the School-Room.

As she started to move along the passage she thought she could hear the sound of music in the distance and knew where it came from.

She had already learned that the guests danced in a room next to the Silver Salon when there was only a small house-party rather than in the big Ball-Room.

'I wish I could see them,' she thought.

The ladies with their full skirts and trains would

look very graceful as they waltzed with the gentlemen in their knee-breeches and evening-coats with tails.

She wondered with whom the Marquis would dance and if he was a good dancer, and was sure that as in everything else he did he would be extremely proficient.

Even as she thought of him she saw the top of his head coming up the main staircase.

She was now in the very centre of the corridor and she stopped still at the sight of him, knowing with a sudden feeling of panic that he must not see her.

She knew he would be curious as to what she was doing in the corridor which led to his own room and where his most distinguished guests were sleeping.

She felt she could not possibly explain that she had gone with one of the house-maids to look at Lady Brooke's clothes.

'What shall I do? Where can I hide?' Lara asked herself desperately.

She thought of running back to Lady Brooke's room, but it was too far away and in one second more the Marquis would have reached the top of the stairs and would come walking down the corridor towards her.

Frantically she turned towards the nearest door and opened it.

She could not remember who Agnes had told her was sleeping there, or whether she had mentioned it at all. She only knew that for the moment it was a hiding place from the Marquis.

As she went inside she found herself in a very small hall and saw two doors opening out of it.

She guessed this was one of the Suites that were arranged on either side of this corridor with a Bedroom and a Sitting-Room for each guest.

She only had a quick glance before she shut the door leading to the corridor, hoping she could stay safely hidden until the Marquis had reached his own rooms, if that was where he was going.

Because she was agitated, she felt her heart beating against her breast and she tried to hold her breath, listening so that she might hear his footsteps pass the door.

Then to her consternation the door was opened and she saw the Marquis's broad shoulders and his figure silhouetted for a moment against the light that came from the silver sconces in the corridor.

Then when she was unable to move or even breathe he shut the door behind him and she was acutely conscious of him standing beside her in the darkness.

Although she could not see him she could feel the vibrations coming from him.

Then astonishingly and surprisingly, so that she could hardly believe it was happening, she felt his arms go round her and he pulled her against him.

Before she could make a sound his lips came down on hers and held her captive.

Lara had never been kissed before and for a moment the touch of the Marquis's mouth seemed unreal, as if it was something which could not be happening and was just part of her imagination.

Then as the pressure of his kiss increased and his arms tightened about her, she felt a strange feeling she had never known before run through her body, through her breasts and up her throat into her lips that were touching his.

It was like a wave, warm and alive with an intensity that was strange and at the same time incredibly wonderful.

Suddenly she knew that this was what she had

longed to feel and it was different from anything she had imagined and was so marvellous that there were no words with which to describe it.

As if the Marquis was aware of what she was feeling and knew the wonder of it, the pressure of his mouth increased.

Now his kiss was more demanding and possessive so that Lara felt as if he drew her heart from her body and made it his, and that she was no longer herself but a part of him.

Because it was impossible to think, but only to feel somewhere far away on a cloud of glory, her mind told her this was love; the love she had sought, the love she wanted, the love that was part of God.

Then when she felt that he had taken her up into the sky, into a special Heaven, and they were no longer human but Divine, he raised his head to say in a voice that sounded curiously unlike his own:

"I must leave you, Daisy. The Prince will be looking for you."

Before Lara could move or even realise what was happening he had taken his arms from her, opened the door, passed through it and shut it behind him.

For a moment she could not think or even realise what had happened. She only knew that her whole body was quivering with the emotions he had evoked in her.

At the same time, she felt as if a life-force was pulsating through her in a manner she had never dreamt possible.

How long she stood there in the darkness feeling her heart thumping within her breast, her breath coming quickly from between her parted lips, she had no idea.

It must in fact have been quite a long time before she felt that her feet were back on the ground and she could breathe naturally.

Then she opened the door and slipped out into the corridor.

Regardless of who might see her, she ran as quickly as she could past the main staircase and along the corridor on the other side of it until she reached the staircase which would lead her up to the School-Room floor.

Only when she could sit down at the table, putting her elbows on it to cover her face with her hands, could she think of what had happened to her and know because the Marquis had kissed her she would never be the same again.

He had awakened her to love and she knew now she had loved him for a long time.

Although he had been incessantly in her thoughts, she had been too inexperienced to know that she had been attracted to him from the very first moment he had spoken to her in the Great Hall.

She had told herself that he was cynical and over-powering but very interesting.

Now she knew he was very much a man; now she could understand why so many women had broken their hearts over him, and why Lady Louise was so unhappy.

'I love him, I love him!' she thought, 'but it is as ridiculous as looking at the moon and longing to reach it. How could I have known that love would be like that and a kiss could be perfect, like touching the rays of the sun?'

She gave a deep sigh and knew that the Marquis must never know what she felt about him, must never have any idea that when he kissed her she had given him not only her lips, but everything she possessed, even her soul.

'He thought he was kissing Lady Brooke,' she said to herself, 'and I suppose he loves her just as the Prince does.'

But she did not want to come back to reality or even try to understand what had happened.

All she could feel whenever she thought of the Marquis was a rapture rising up within her, and the memory of how his lips had held her captive, and the strength of his arms.

She knew too there was a strange vibration between them that had made them closer even than the touch of their bodies, because it came from within themselves and was not physical, but utterly and completely spiritual.

"I love him!" Lara said aloud.

She wondered what he would say or think if he knew it had not been Lady Brooke he had been kissing at that moment but a Governess, an inferior being of no consequence, despite the fact that he admired the way she rode.

She sat for a long time at the table before she came to a decision.

'I will go home! The Marquis must never know what I feel about him. If I stay here too long I might betray myself inadvertently because I could not help it.'

She thought how contemptuous he would look, how presumptuous he would think it, if he knew her feelings for him.

She was also certain that the cynical lines on his face would deepen if he thought she was another importunate female for whom he had no use, but who loved him.

'I must go away,' she told herself.

And yet the idea of leaving was as painful as if she had stabbed her breast with a dagger, because it would mean she would never see the Marquis again.

Because it was hard to contemplate a lifetime without him and with only the memory of his kiss, she rose from the table restlessly, thinking that tonight she could not even set down on paper what had occurred or what she had felt.

'I will go to bed,' she decided and walked towards the School-Room door to lock it.

As she put out her hand towards it she realised something was missing.

It was the key!

She looked at the lock as if she could not believe what she saw, but the key was not there.

A sudden thought struck her and she walked quickly to her bedroom door but even before she reached it she knew what she would find.

The key to that door was also missing.

Then she knew that the moment she had anticipated would come sooner or later had arrived. Here was the confrontation with Lord Magor that she had expected before she came to the Priory.

Just for a moment she felt panic-stricken. She could not face him, could not bear, when her whole body was throbbing with the wonder of the Marquis's kiss, to fight and defy a man she despised and loathed.

It flashed through her mind that she could run upstairs to Nanny and ask for her protection.

Then she knew she would not demean herself to do anything so feeble.

Instead she would teach Lord Magor the lesson she had intended when she learned how he had frightened Jane.

'I am not a helpless orphan with no parents to protect me,' she told herself, 'and afraid of losing my employment.'

She knew her father could speak to Lord Magor on equal terms and tell him if necessary what a cad he was.

Yet she knew she had no wish to worry her father and she wanted to deal with Lord Magor herself.

Pride came to her rescue, and lifting her chin she walked to her trunk which stood in a corner of her bedroom and which she had instructed the house-maids was not to be taken away.

She opened it and from the bottom, hidden under some clothes which had not been unpacked, she drew out one of the duelling pistols which had belonged to her great-grandfather.

Only to touch it made her feel that the courage he had always shown was transmitting itself to her.

Now she was not really frightened, only a little apprehensive and aware that her heart was beating tumultuously but not in the exciting and wonderful way it had done when the Marquis had put his arms around her.

She loaded the pistol, cocked it, and holding it steady in her right hand walked back into the Sitting-Room.

She glanced at the clock on the mantelpiece and saw that she had sat so long at the table thinking about the Marquis and the ecstasy he had aroused in her that it was later than she expected.

She was sure that Lord Magor would soon come to her, confident that this time he would have his way.

144

She thought how terrified Jane would be if she were here now, and she knew that whatever Lord Magor would have done to her, although Lara was not quite certain what it would be, the result would be that Jane would collapse completely and be ill perhaps for months.

'No man could be more wicked than to torture anyone so helpless and weak as Jane,' she told herself.

She remembered the question that Georgina had asked earlier in the day—wasn't it wicked to be cruel to something small and helpless—and knew the child had been absolutely right, and it was something she was now prepared to revenge.

She sat down at the table, put the pistol in her lap, aware as she did so that although she had not thought of it before, she was wearing the pretty blue evening-gown which was Jane's.

Somehow tonight it had seemed suitable that when she watched the house-party going down to dinner she should wear her best, just as they were wearing theirs.

It was a childish idea, but when Lara looked at herself in the mirror she had known that Jane's gown, which was cut quite low at the neck, was exceedingly becoming.

It was made only of a cheap material, but in a very pretty shade of blue, and was trimmed with chiffon which encircled the décolletage to frame Lara's white shoulders and long neck.

It suddenly struck her that Lord Magor might think she had put on her best gown to receive him, and she thought in that case he would have an extremely unpleasant surprise.

The minutes seemed to pass slowly, but Lara had in fact only waited for a little over a quarter-of-an-hour when she heard footsteps coming up the stairs.

She was aware that Lord Magor was deliberately walking lightly so as not to be heard.

She wondered if he was smiling in the way she detested, a smile of triumph because he knew she had no defences left and whatever feeble resistance she might put up, he would have his way.

The door opened and he stood for a moment looking at her as she sat at the table, her head held high, the light glinting on her hair, making it a halo of flame.

For a moment there was silence. Then Lord Magor smiled.

"Good-evening!" he said. "I imagine you were expecting me."

"I was, My Lord. I could not believe that anybody else in the house would be likely to remove the keys from both these doors."

"Without them I could not come in," Lord Magor argued, entering the room and shutting the door behind him. "And now, my lovely little disciplinarian, there is no need to play games and I will prove to you that the lessons I shall teach you will be very enjoyable."

"Suppose I ask you as a gentleman to leave me alone?" Lara suggested.

"At the moment I am not a gentleman," Lord Magor replied, "but a man who finds you very alluring with your red hair and your white skin which excites me more than I can tell you in words."

He drew a little nearer as he said:

"But words are unnecessary between us, and it is much easier for me to tell you what I feel and what I will make you feel when we are close to each other."

He took another step and Lara rose to her feet, the pistol in her hand.

146

She moved away from the table, saying as she did so:

"That is far enough, My Lord! And now let me tell you what I think of you!"

She saw the astonishment in Lord Magor's eyes as he saw the pistol and she went on:

"I despise and detest you! I would rather be touched by the lowest reptile that crawls than by you. I intend to make sure that you will never again molest helpless young Governesses who cannot defend themselves as I am able to do."

Because she was very angry she almost spat the words at him and there was first of all a glint of anger in Lord Magor's eyes. Then he laughed.

"Bravely spoken!" he said. "But you are not fool enough to jeopardise your position here or in any other house by shooting me."

He paused as if he was weighing up his words before he uttered them. Then he added:

"If you fire that ridiculous weapon you have in your hand, you know as well as I do that no one would ever employ you again. Then, my pretty one, you would starve, unless I looked after you—which I am quite prepared to do."

Lara was pointing the gun at him with a steady hand and he did not move as he said almost coaxingly:

"Stop playing the Amazon and let me tell you what I have in mind: a comfortable little house in St. John's Wood, a horse and carriage of your own, and jewels— I think emeralds to make your skin look even whiter than it does at the moment."

It seemed to Lara there was a fire in his eyes and in his voice as he said:

"Let me touch it, and I promise you shall have

anything, not just one emerald, but a necklace of them."

"I would rather starve!" Lara exclaimed.

"Nonsense!" Lord Magor replied. "I will give you a life that is more enjoyable than anything you have ever imagined."

He stepped forward as he spoke.

"Keep away!" Lara said warningly.

"I want to hold you in my arms," Lord Magor answered.

He came nearer still.

It was then Lara fired at him. She had meant to aim at his arm, not his heart, but as she pulled the trigger she felt the duelling pistol kick upwards.

In the explosion which followed, which seemed to echo and re-echo round the walls, she thought for a moment she had missed him.

Then slowly, so slowly that it was somehow more frightening than if it had happened quickly, Lord Magor's hands clutched at his chest, then he collapsed and fell backwards onto the carpet.

For a second Lara could not move. She could only stand staring at the fallen man.

She saw that his face was bloodless and his eyes were closed.

It was then that a feeling of horror over what she had done swept over her. She had killed him instead of, as she had intended, wounding him in the arm and the repercussions of her act would be terrible.

She felt as if her brain were filled with sawdust.

She was deaf from the sound of the explosion and it was hard to breathe, but she knew that as Lord Magor was dead the police would have to be brought in, and nothing could be more disastrous when the Prince of Wales was in the house.

There had been scandals about him before and the

newspapers had flayed him for his extravagance, for his friends, and for his way of life which had incurred the displeasure of the Queen and a great number of her subjects as well.

It flashed through Lara's mind now that the Marquis would be censured for allowing anything so disgraceful as a murder to happen at the Priory, especially when the Prince was a guest.

Because she loved him she knew she would do anything at this moment to put back the clock and have Lord Magor standing on his feet even if, as he had intended, he touched her.

'I should not have stayed here when I found the keys were missing,' she thought.

But it was too late! Lord Magor was lying dead at her feet and the Marquis would never forgive her.

Moreover, he would hate to have it known that his closest friend was attempting to seduce a woman he employed to teach his niece. The publicity would infuriate him.

It all seemed to flash through Lara's mind like a streak of lightning.

She realised that she must somehow save the Marquis from the consequences of her crime, but how to do so she had no idea.

She put the pistol down on the table, then walking round the body of Lord Magor she reached the door.

It was then she knew there was only one person who could help her; one person who perhaps by some miracle might prevent the consequences of her crime from being as catastrophic as she now thought they must be.

Without stopping, without even thinking of what she should say or how she should explain her action, she knew that she must find the Marquis and ask his help.

Without looking back she went down the stairs, reached the next floor, then ran as swiftly as she could along the corridor which stretched almost the whole length of the building.

As she reached the Marquis's room, because she had run so fast she stopped for a moment to catch her breath.

Her heart was beating so wildly that she felt it might burst from her breast, her lips were dry and her hands were trembling.

Nevertheless she opened the door and found herself in a small hall like the one where the Marquis had kissed her.

There was a low light burning which showed her two doors at either side of it.

Without thinking, without even knocking, she opened the nearest one and as the light from where she was standing percolated a little way into the room she could see very faintly the posts of a great bed.

Then as she stood indecisive, feeling as if her voice had died in her throat, she heard the Marquis ask:

"Who is it? What do you want?"

Because she was so glad he was there she moved swiftly towards him.

She was silhouetted against the light and he was therefore able to recognise her.

As she reached the side of the bed he exclaimed, and she could hear the incredulous note in his voice:

"Miss Wade!"

For a moment Lara thought she could not speak. Then in a voice which seemed to come from a long, long way away she stammered:

"I...I am...sorry...terribly...terribly sorry... but I have...shot Lord...Magor...and he is...dead!"

chapter seven

THERE was what seemed to be a long silence, while
aware that Lara was trembling the Marquis knew she
was speaking the truth.

He said quietly and calmly:

"Wait outside the door. I will not be a minute."

Feeling almost as if her legs would not carry her,
Lara turned towards the lighted door and went into
the small hall.

She stood with her back to the Marquis's room
and, because the door was ajar, she could hear him
moving about and knew he had turned on the light.

She waited, feeling as if she was sinking lower and
lower into the ground and that when she reached the
bottom of some unfathomable pit, she would die.

It was what she wanted to do, knowing that in
killing Lord Magor she had hurt the Marquis irretriev-
ably, for his guest's murder—it was nothing else—

would have repercussions which would be known to everyone in the country.

"How could I have been so foolish?" she asked.

She wished she had been brave enough to tell the Marquis what Lord Magor was like and how he had terrified Jane and then transferred his desires to herself.

But even if he was wicked, that was no excuse for her creating a scandal when the Prince of Wales was staying in the house.

It seemed to Lara at that moment as if she was the guilty one and that if anyone should be punished it was she.

She could only have stood in the small, dimly lighted hall for perhaps two or three minutes, but it seemed to her, as if to a drowning man, that all the past flashed before her eyes and accused her of being a criminal.

Then the Marquis joined her.

She saw he was fully dressed, except that instead of a collar and tie there was a scarf round his neck, which gave him a somewhat raffish look.

Without speaking he opened the outer door and they started to walk down the corridor side by side.

The only light was from the candles spluttering low in the sconces.

Although some parts of the Priory had the new, much vaunted electricity and some gas-lighting, in the principal rooms and in the main corridors the Marquis kept to the traditional candles.

These stood in the sconces which, Lara had been told, had been made for the house in the reign of Charles II by one of the great silversmiths of the time.

All she was aware of now was that the corridor seemed dim, and she felt as if she was walking in a fog of her own making and she would never know the light of happiness again.

They passed the door behind which she had hidden earlier in the evening and where the Marquis had kissed her, thinking her to be Lady Brooke.

For one moment Lara felt a little surge of remembrance creep into her breast as she recalled the wonder and glory of his lips, the way in which he had carried her into the sky and they seemed to touch the divine.

But she told herself bitterly that she had betrayed her love and was now unworthy of the rapture that she had known for one brief moment but which could never be hers again.

Only as they passed the main staircase and reached the passage which led to the West Wing, did the Marquis say:

"Where is Lord Magor?"

"In the . . . School-Room," Lara managed to reply.

"Why was he there?"

There was a pause before Lara answered:

"He . . . came to . . . see me."

"You were waiting for him?"

The question was sharp and she thought the Marquis's voice was contemptuous.

She was looking ahead but she thought he glanced at her and was aware she was wearing evening dress.

It was an added horror to what she was feeling to know he was suspecting her of deliberately inviting Lord Magor's attentions. Because she could not bear him to think such a thing, she said quickly:

"I was . . . waiting because he had . . . removed the keys from the door of the . . . School-Room and from my . . . bedroom."

The Marquis stopped and turned to look at her searchingly.

"Is this true?"

"He tried to get in...last night," Lara replied, "but I had locked the door. He...had to go...away."

She saw the Marquis's lips tighten before he said:

"So tonight you waited with the intention to shoot him?"

"Yes!"

There was a little pause before he asked:

"With one of my guns?"

It was difficult for Lara to reply and she realised it would have to lead to other explanations. There was nothing she could do but answer:

"No...I had a ...duelling pistol which...belonged to my...father."

"You brought it here with you when you arrived to teach Georgina? Why?"

She thought he was being clever in extracting from her the whole story so quickly, and she wanted to say that instead of talking they should go upstairs and find Lord Magor.

Yet as if he held her prisoner and she was in the dock, she could only give him the answer for which he was waiting.

In a low voice so that he could hardly hear, she said:

"I brought...the pistol with me...because I knew what...Lord Magor was...like."

"How did you know that?" the Marquis asked.

Then before she could reply, he added:

"I presume you must have heard of him from Miss Cooper."

"Yes...and she was...terrified of him. That was why I...took her place...so that she could have a...holiday."

"You mean she was not really ill?"

"No ... only frightened to the point where I ... thought she might have a ... nervous breakdown."

The Marquis drew in his breath and she knew he was angry, very angry.

He did not say anything but merely walked on, and there was nothing she could do but walk after him until they reached the staircase which led up to the next floor.

He climbed it ahead of her and as he reached first the landing and then the door which led into the School-Room, Lara found herself praying that somehow by some miracle Lord Magor would have disappeared.

But when she looked into the room, she could see his body lying where she had left it and knew that her prayers had failed and her last hope had gone.

It was then that she heard a cry from Georgina's room.

Without waiting and as the Marquis stopped to bend over the body of the dead man, she ran towards Georgina's bedroom door and opened it.

"Miss Wade! Miss Wade!" Georgina was calling as she entered.

Quickly Lara shut the door behind her and groped her way to the bedside, feeling for the matches, saying as she did so:

"It's all right, darling, I am here!"

"I heard a big bang," Georgina said. "I thought perhaps they were shooting the poor baby foxes."

With difficulty, because her fingers were trembling, Lara lit a candle and then she sat down on the edge of the mattress facing Georgina.

"I think you must have been dreaming," she said. "It is far too dark outside for the Keepers to shoot anything at this time of night."

"I called and called but you did not come," Georgina said reproachfully.

"I am sorry, dearest, I am sorry!" Lara answered. "But I did not hear you."

"I was . . . frightened!"

"There is nothing to frighten you now I am here."

"No, not now," Georgina said. "But it is horrid being frightened in the dark."

"Yes, I know," Lara answered. "So I am going to teach you a prayer my mother taught me when I was younger than you and which I want you to say if ever again you are frightened in the night."

"Is it a magic prayer?"

"I have always found it very magic," Lara answered.

The child cuddled down against the pillow and Lara pulled the sheet up to her chin.

Then she said very softly the prayer which was so much a part of her childhood that she felt almost as if she could hear her mother's voice saying it to her.

"Lighten our darkness, we beseech Thee, O Lord; and by Thy great mercy defend us from all perils and dangers of this night; for the love of Thy only Son, our Saviour, Jesus Christ. Amen."

By the time she had finished Georgina's eyes were closing and then, as Lara waited, she said drowsily:

"That is . . . magic and I shall . . . always say . . . it . . ."

There was silence and after a few seconds Lara knew she was asleep.

She waited until she was quite certain that if she moved she would not disturb the child, then she blew out the candle and walked on tip-toe towards the door, guided by the light which came from beneath it.

She went into the School-Room to find it empty.

There was no sign of the Marquis and Lord Magor was no longer lying on the floor.

The Marquis, she supposed, must have carried him away, and the only evidence left of the crime was that her father's duelling pistol was where she had left it on the table.

She picked it up, carried it into her bedroom, and hid it in the bottom of her trunk. As she did so she wondered if perhaps until the trial the police would allow her to go home or whether she would be taken to prison immediately.

The idea was so terrifying that she wanted to scream, but instead she could only stand with her hands on her breast as if to stop the beating of her heart.

Her father would have to know what she had done and, although he would support and sustain her, she knew he would be deeply distressed.

Jane, poor frightened Jane, would undoubtedly have to give evidence that she had told her about Lord Magor, which was why she had brought duelling pistols with her to the Priory.

"How could I have ever thought of doing anything so crazy, so idiotic?" Lara asked desperately. "Oh, Mama, help me! Help me!"

She cried out to her mother as a child might have done, and indeed at that moment she felt she was no older than Georgina.

She wanted to cry in her mother's arms.

Then insidiously, so that she could not prevent it, the thought came creeping into her mind that, since her mother was dead, there was only one other place where she could feel safe and that was if the Marquis held her as he had done when he kissed her.

She wanted to cry because she was well aware what he must think of her now.

Because she could not bear to see the condemnation in his eyes or hear him say how much he despised her, she wanted to run away immediately, so that she would never need see him again.

But she knew that wherever she ran she would be fetched back and brought to justice.

She gave a little murmur of pain, mingled with contrition and horror, and put her hands up to her eyes. As she did so she heard a sound in the School-Room and knew the Marquis had come back.

There was nothing that she could do but go to him and face what was coming to her.

It flashed through her mind that she must not whine or complain, but should behave with the same dignity that he would show in any circumstances however dramatic.

Slowly, because it demanded an almost superhuman effort, she turned and walked into the next room.

The Marquis was waiting for her, standing with his back to the fireplace.

She could not look at him, but went to the table and stood with her hands resting on it because she was desperately in need of support.

Once again she was trembling. She knew that her face must be very pale because she felt all the blood had left it. Yet she managed to hold her head high, although her eyes were downcast.

There was a little pause before the Marquis said in a low voice, as if he was afraid of disturbing Georgina:

"I have taken Lord Magor to his room. He is not dead."

For a moment what he had said did not percolate her mind, and then she thought she could not have heard him aright.

She stiffened and her eyes were on his.

"Did you . . . say he is . . . not . . . dead," she whispered.

The Marquis nodded.

"Yes! He is alive and actually your bullet did not touch him."

"It cannot be . . . true," Lara faltered. "When I fired he . . . collapsed and his . . . hands went to his . . . chest."

Her words were almost incoherent but her eyes were still on the Marquis's face, looking at his searchingly as if she thought for some reason she could not understand he was lying to her.

"He collapsed with a heart-attack," the Marquis said quietly. "He has suffered from his heart for some time and I have given him the medicine he always carries with him. He is now conscious and I have sent a groom for the doctor."

"Is this . . . true? Is it . . . really . . . true?" Lara asked.

"I think you know it is."

She sat down suddenly on the chair, as if her legs could no longer carry her.

"I was so . . . sure he was . . . dead," she said almost as if she spoke to herself. "I thought I would . . . have to . . . face a trial for . . . murder."

"No one is to have any idea what has happened here tonight," the Marquis said sharply. "You must keep everything to yourself and not speak of it, do you understand?"

She thought his voice was hard and unsympathetic.

At the same time she felt as if life was coming

back into her body and into her mind and it was she rather than Lord Magor who had come back from the dead.

In a kinder tone, as if he understood, the Marquis went on:

"Go to bed! Everything will seem better in the morning. I will deal with everything."

As he finished speaking he looked at her for a long moment, almost as if he thought she might faint. Then, re-assured, he walked across the room and left the School-Room, closing the door behind him.

It was only when she could no longer hear his footsteps down the stairs that Lara stretched out her arms on the table and put her head down on them.

She had been saved by a miracle and perhaps by her mother's prayers, but she knew only too well what the Marquis was thinking of her.

She sat for a long time at the table before she rose and, going into her bedroom, began to pack her trunk.

*　　*　　*

"I don't say that Miss Cooper couldn't have done with another week to put the roses in her cheeks," Nanny said. "The rest has certainly done her good, which is more than I can say for you, Miss Lara."

"I am just tired after the journey," Lara said quickly. "I had to leave very early in the morning."

"Well, you might have let the Master know you were coming," Nanny said, "and he'd have met you at the station."

"Farmer Jackson was there and he gave me a lift home," Lara answered.

Nanny knew this already, but Lara wanted to keep talking to prevent her asking too many questions as to why she had returned so unexpectedly.

She told Jane the reason when they were alone.

"You can go back to the Priory now, Jane," she said. "Lord Magor has had a heart-attack. I expect he will be ill for some time."

"That is good news," Jane said. "You did not have any trouble with him?"

"He was not interested in me," Lara replied, hoping she would be forgiven for telling a lie.

"I was worried, very worried."

"Before you go back," Lara said, "I want to tell you what I have discovered about Georgina."

She told her how musical the child was and how the Marquis intended to find the best teachers for her.

"In which case they will not want me," Jane said quickly. "I cannot play the piano and I have never liked music."

"You can teach Georgina all her other lessons," Lara said. "But actually, Jane, I think you would be happier with younger children."

"Perhaps I would," Jane agreed, "and I do not think anyone would mind if I left the Priory. Perhaps I could put my name down with one of the Domestic Bureaux which cater for Governesses."

She did not sound very enthusiastic about it and Lara said:

"I think you would be wiser to ask Lady Ludlow if she knows any of her friends with young children who need someone like you. Or, if you would like, I will ask Papa to write to her, since she is a relation."

"That would be very, very kind of you," Jane replied. Then she added, "I think perhaps I ought to go back this afternoon. I could stay the night at Keyston House in London. I am sure they will make arrangements to send me in a carriage to the Priory first thing tomorrow morning."

"That is a good idea," Lara said. "I left a note for

Georgina, telling her that you would be coming back. I am sure she will be looking forward to seeing you."

This, again, was another lie. She was quite certain that Georgina would miss her, especially as there would be no-one to ride with her except a groom.

She had told the child she had to go home because her father needed her urgently and told her to be very kind to Miss Cooper after she had been ill.

She had also asked her to explain to her uncle that she had not been able to say good-bye because she had had to leave so early.

She ended:

> *"You must go on working hard at your music, Dearest, because I know you are going to be very, very good at it, and I will be thinking of you and praying for you. When you have time write to me and tell me all the things that you are doing. You know I shall want to hear from you.*
>
> My love and God bless you,
Lara Wade"

When she had finished writing the note, she had left it outside Georgina's bedroom door, knowing that Nanny would take it in when she called her in the morning.

Lara had then dressed herself in her travelling-clothes and waited until she had heard the stable-yard bell ring at six o'clock.

She had gone downstairs and asked the first foot-man she saw, looking sleepy and in his shirt-sleeves, to go to the stables to say she requested a carriage to take her to the station.

When he returned she had told him to bring down her trunk.

There was no sign of any of the older servants when she left the Priory a quarter-of-an-hour later. The young ones merely obeyed her orders and were not curious enough to ask why she was leaving.

It was all much easier than she had expected. She had caught a train which steamed into the station only ten minutes after she had arrived there.

She had, however, a long wait in London before there was a train to take her, stopping at every station, to the Halt for Little Fladbury.

But she was home. In contrast to the Priory, the Vicarage looked even smaller, more shabby and threadbare than it had before.

She had tried not to think of anything except making Jane believe that, since now she was safe from Lord Magor, her job was waiting for her and her place was with Georgina.

Lara had driven Jane to the station, because her father had returned with Rollo and the trap was available.

But after the train had gone Lara felt so exhausted that when she reached home she lay down on her bed and instantly fell asleep.

When she woke it was dinner time. But she looked so white-faced and limp that Nanny would not let her get up but insisted on bringing her a dish of scrambled eggs and a glass of milk.

After she had finished them, Lara undressed, got into bed, and went to sleep again.

*   *   *

It was only in the morning, when Lara woke as the sun came streaming through the thin curtains which covered the windows, that she could think of her love for the Marquis and realise that she had lost him for ever.

It was an'agony which tore her to pieces.

'How can I bear it?' she asked. 'To live here for the rest of my life, thinking of him, longing for him, and knowing I was right when I thought he was as out of reach as the moon.'

And yet for one moment she had been close to him and, although he might deny it and it meant nothing to him, she had become a part of him.

It had changed, transformed her so that she could never be the same again.

"I love him! I love him!" she whispered as she lay in the narrow bed in which she had slept ever since she had been too big to use a cot.

She could see his face in front of her eyes, almost as if he stood in the room beside her.

She wondered what he would think when he learnt that she had gone, but she knew that he would be relieved now there would be no awkwardness to encounter when Lord Magor was better.

She had the feeling that perhaps the Marquis might have made him apologise for his behaviour and that would have been an embarrassment she could not contemplate, or, worse still, if the Marquis had apologised for his friend.

She would also have to confess more fully her contrition in having been so foolish as to take the law into her own hands and shoot at a man who, however he behaved, was still a guest of her employer and under the same roof as the Prince of Wales.

'It was all crazy,' she thought, 'and part of a world that only exists in my imagination and has nothing to do with reality.'

When she unpacked her trunk she found her manuscript books, but suddenly she had no wish to go on writing the novel which had absorbed her up to now.

What was the point of trying to tell a tale about people who, even though she had seen them and heard about them, were so far removed from her own thinking and feeling that she could never make them seem real and human to the reader?

'I will write a book,' she told herself, 'which will be about country people, of whom I know a great deal, not about Society, with its strange code of behaviour and which would be better left unknown to people outside their own special circle.'

* * *

"It is nice to have you back, dear child," her father said the next day, as they had breakfast together.

When he said the same at luncheon, Lara knew he had genuinely missed her.

"I love being with you, Papa!" she answered. "I have no wish to go away again."

"I was glad for you to have a change all the same," Lord Hurlington said, "for I am well aware, darling, how dull it must be for you here. I wish I had the chance of moving, but I think, if the truth were known, the Bishop has forgotten I even exist."

"We are very happy in Little Fladbury," Lara said loyally, "and everyone here loves you, Papa, as you well know."

At the same time it passed through her mind that the Marquis must have many livings on his vast Estates.

It would be so easy, if he were willing, to appoint her father to a much bigger Parish with a far larger stipend. But she thought bitterly that that was something which would never happen!

Although she tried to busy herself about the house, she could not help wondering what was happening at the Priory and if the Marquis even gave her so much as a passing thought.

She lay awake thinking of him all that night, and when Monday came she knew the Prince of Wales and Lady Brooke and all the rest of the guests would leave in a flurry of "good-byes."

A mountain of trunks would be carried downstairs and placed on the brakes which would take them with the lady's-maids, valets, and other servants to the station.

The Prince, Lady Brooke, and some of their more intimate friends would travel on the Royal train.

She wondered if the Marquis would go with them or perhaps because he might want to ride *Black Knight* or one of his other superlative horses, he would stay until later in the day.

She imagined that he and Georgina would go to the race-course and wondered if they would miss her and if Georgina would say, as she had done before, that it was more fun with three horses.

'I have to forget; I cannot go on thinking about it like this,' Lara told herself severely.

She put on her bonnet, the old one, which was all she possessed, Jane having taken the one with blue ribbons back with her to the Priory, and set off down to the village.

There was an elderly woman whom she often called on when she had the time, and who was growing blind and could only sit in her small cottage waiting for a kind neighbour to tell her what was happening in the world outside.

Lara had picked a few sprigs of fragrant white lilac

in the garden, which was coming into bloom.

These, of course, made her think of the shrubs at the Priory through which she had walked when she heard Lady Louise saying how much she loved the Marquis.

If Lady Louise had joined the list of women who had loved and lost him, so had she. Only he would never know about it and would certainly not have her complaining or arriving, as Lady Louise had, as an unwanted guest.

'The Marquis is lucky on that count,' she told herself bitterly.

She spent an hour with the blind woman, and because it was difficult to talk of anything else she told her about the Priory and Georgina. Although she tried not to mention the Marquis, somehow his name crept into the story.

When she rose to say good-bye, the old woman held her hand in both of hers and said:

"You've been hurt, dearie, I can hear it in your voice. I pray things'll come right for you. God often listens to my prayers."

"I am sure He does," Lara answered.

"And you'll find happiness—that I know in my heart. You're a good girl and like your mother. There was never a finer or kinder lady than her."

"That is true," Lara said, "and thank you for saying I am like her."

"She was happy, very happy with your father, and you'll be happy too and don't forget I told you so."

"I will not forget."

Lara thought she spoke of the happiness she wanted but which would never come to her.

She walked back along the dusty road which

twisted between the small thatched cottages and passed the village green before there was the first sight of the grey stone Church.

But she was seeing the velvet lawns slipping down to the stream, where once the Monks had fished, and the rose pink of the Priory walls, and the Great Hall with its beamed ceiling, where she had first met the Marquis.

Try as she would she could not escape him and she knew he filled her mind and her heart.

It was no use to fight against love, and even if she could not reach the moon, she could look at it and know that it was there in the sky.

She opened the Vicarage door and left it open to let in the sunshine. She knew her father was out visiting a farm, where the wife of the farmer was very ill.

Nanny was shopping in the village and though Lara had seen her in the distance she had not stopped but walked on.

She preferred her own thoughts to Nanny's endless questions as to why she looked so pale and would eat practically nothing since she had returned home.

She went into the Sitting-Room and knew that what she should do now was to go into the garden and try to pick enough flowers to make it look more spring-like.

She pulled off her bonnet and put it down on a chair, and then went to the window to look out over the untidy garden.

As she did so she was thinking once again of the Priory and its beauty, which had moved her as the music did which she had played to Georgina.

Strangely, she thought she missed the child almost as much as she missed the Marquis. She had never had much to do with children. Now she knew she would love above all things to have a child of her own.

Yet motherhood was something she would never know because it was impossible to marry a man she did not love.

'The Marquis has ruined my life,' she thought with a little twist of her lips. 'He has even taken my dreams from me.'

Behind her she heard footsteps in the hall and then the door opened. She turned expectantly, thinking that Nanny must have returned from the village.

Then she was suddenly still.

It was not Nanny in her shawl and bonnet who stood in the doorway but the Marquis, looking very smart and very large. He seemed somehow to fill the whole of the small Sitting-Room until his head touched the ceiling.

Lara gave a little gasp.

Then suddenly afraid she asked, the words seeming to pour out of her lips:

"What has ... happened? Why are you ... here? Is ... something ... wrong?"

It flashed through her mind that perhaps Lord Magor had died after all and that she was responsible for it.

The Marquis shut the door behind him and walked towards her.

"Nothing is wrong," he said. "Except I could not believe you would leave without telling me you were doing so."

Just because he was there, or perhaps because there was a note in his voice which she did not understand, Lara felt her heart begin to thump in her breast.

The Marquis reached her side and stood looking

down at her. The sun coming through the window brought out the red in her hair.

"Why did you leave?" he asked.

"I thought you would not . . . want me to stay . . . after what I had . . . done."

"You might at least have asked me what I wished you to do," he said quietly.

As he was standing so close to her Lara was afraid, since she could feel the vibrations coming from him, that he would feel hers reaching out towards him and be aware of how much she loved him.

She felt as if her whole body was singing because she could see him, but she told herself he would be shocked and perhaps horrified if he knew how glad she was.

He gave her the feeling that her whole being was tingling with the life-force, which was also love.

"Georgina was deeply distressed when she found you had left," the Marquis said.

"I am sorry, I did not . . . mean to . . . upset her," Lara replied quickly. "I sent Miss Cooper back."

"Miss Cooper does not ride as you do, nor is she in the least musical."

"You promised to find music teachers for Georgina."

"I shall do that, but Georgina asked me to beg you to come back."

He was speaking in a quiet, deep voice, and it seemed as if there was something very intimate about it. Lara felt almost as if he spoke to music.

She was trying to think what she should say and somehow the truth came to her lips:

"I am not . . . really a . . . Governess."

"I know that," the Marquis replied. "I forced Miss Cooper to tell me exactly who you were."

"You were not unkind to her?" Lara asked without thinking.

"I hope not," the Marquis replied, "but I cannot help it if she is terrified of me, can I?"

There was a hint of amusement in his voice as he added:

"As you never were!"

"I was frightened that you would be . . . angry after I had . . . shot Lord Magor."

"Not very effectively," the Marquis replied. "Perhaps your effectiveness as a marksman needs a great deal more practice."

Now he was undoubtedly amused. Lara glanced up at him to ask:

"You are not . . . angry with . . . me?"

"Not in the least," the Marquis replied. "He thoroughly deserved it. But if you had told me what he was doing, I could have punished him far more effectively than you were able to do."

"How could you do that?" Lara asked in surprise.

"By making sure he is never again invited to the Priory or any of the other houses I own," the Marquis answered.

"Do you mean that? Do you really mean that?" she asked. "I am glad, so very glad. It has worried me to think that Governesses, who are so vulnerable and so helpless, can be persecuted by men like that."

She spoke without thinking and wondered if she had said too much.

But there was a smile on the Marquis's lips and she thought it was not the cynical, mocking one, but for some strange reason which she could not understand he looked happy.

There was silence and then he said:

"Now, Lord Magor having been disposed of, what

do you intend to do about Georgina and of course—
me?"

Lara's eyes widened and she asked a little helplessly:

"What . . . can I do?"

"We want you to come back to the Priory."

She was about to ask how she could do that, when
he said quietly:

"Not as a Governess but in a much more permanent
position."

Lara drew in her breath and the expression in her
eyes was still questioning. The Marquis put out his
arms and drew her close to him.

"Shall we find out," he asked in a voice that
sounded somewhat strange, "if our second kiss is as
wonderful as the first?"

He did not wait for an answer. His lips came down
on hers.

As she felt the wonder of it shoot through her like
a shaft of sunlight, she thought this could not be true
and that she was dreaming.

Yet the ecstasy she had felt before was already
rising within her, moving from her throat to her lips
and her whole body vibrated with the glory of it.

As if the Marquis felt the same, he held her closer
still and his kiss became more demanding, more passionate and possessive.

Once again he was carrying her into the sky, the
Heavens opened for them and they were one, not with
the moon but with the burning power of the sun.

It enveloped them with a light that was blinding
and which came not only from the sun itself but from
within them both.

The Marquis kissed her until she was breathless
and as thrill after thrill pulsated through her, she felt

it was impossible to feel such rapture and not die from it.

Only when he raised his head could she say incoherently:

"I love...you! I love...you! I know I must be... dreaming...please...kiss me again...in case I... wake up."

He gave a little laugh, which was curiously unsteady and then he kissed her until Lara felt he possessed her completely.

A long time later the Marquis drew Lara to the sofa and they sat down side by side, his arms around her.

"Shall we make plans, my lovely one?" he asked.

"It is...hard for me to think of...anything except that you...love me. I love you so desperately," Lara answered, "I cannot...believe it possible for...you to...love me...why should you?"

"I can give you an answer to that," the Marquis replied. "When I first saw you standing in the Great Hall I thought you were the most beautiful person I had ever seen in my life. The red of your hair challenged me like a little flag of defiance, and I knew I wanted you."

Lara made a murmur of happiness and he went on:

"But my very critical, very fastidious brain put to me the same question as you have just asked, and I told myself that Governesses were not my concern and I must have drunk too much wine the night before."

"Yet you...kissed me," Lara whispered.

"How could I help it?" he replied. "I saw you disappearing into the room where I knew no-one was sleeping and I was aware you were hiding from me."

His arms tightened round her as he continued:

"I intended to ask you what you were doing in that particular corridor when you should have been in the School-Room, but when I was aware you were hiding in the darkness I could no longer control my need for you."

"It was wonderful...more...wonderful than I ever...knew a kiss...could be, but you thought I was...Lady Brooke."

"I only said that to protect myself from my own feelings."

"You...knew it was...me."

"Do you think I could kiss you and it could be utterly and completely marvellous besides being different to any kiss I have ever known and I would not be aware who I was kissing?"

"It...it...was...marvellous for...me."

"You had never been kissed before?"

"No!"

"I was sure of it," the Marquis said, "so sure, my darling, I was counting the hours until my guests left and I could kiss you again."

Lara leant her head against his shoulder.

"I thought you would be...shocked because I had been...looking at the...beautiful gowns owned by Lady Brooke."

She felt as she spoke that she was confessing something reprehensible. At the same time she had to be truthful.

"You shall have far more beautiful ones," the Marquis smiled, "and yet you are so lovely, my precious, that I adore you just as you look now."

"I felt so ashamed of my clothes and my habit," Lara whispered.

The Marquis laughed.

"You are really a woman at heart. Sometimes when

you argued with me and defied me, I was afraid you were not feminine, but one of those modern women who want to dominate men."

"I would never attempt to . . . dominate you," Lara answered. "At the same time I love arguing with you. It is stimulating in a way I cannot explain."

"It stimulates me too," the Marquis said. "Ever since I met you, my darling, I have known why other women have bored me. It is because I have always been aware of what they were about to say before they said it!"

He kissed her forehead before he finished:

"Instead of inspiring me or, as you say, stimulating me, they have merely acted mentally as a sedative."

Lara gave a little laugh and then she said:

"Supposing after a . . . little while you are . . . bored with me? You do realise that because I am very . . . ignorant of your world and have never done any of the social things which you do . . . you will have thrown away your . . . freedom and gained . . . nothing."

"I shall have gained you," the Marquis said, "and that is all I want. While I realise, as Miss Cooper has told me, that you are very poor and you have lived here all your life, you have thought about so many things and that I shall find it impossible to be bored with you. And what is more, I have a great deal to teach you."

"You . . . want to do . . . that?"

"I want more than anything else to teach you about love. Apart from that we have a great deal in common, our horses, and, please God, in time our children."

He watched the blush that coloured Lara's cheeks and then he said:

"When I watched you listening to Georgina playing the piano and willing me to appreciate her talent, I knew that was what I wanted you to feel about our own daughters and sons."

Lara drew in her breath and again she hid her face against him, as she said:

"I love Georgina. I know now I would adore to have . . . children of . . . my own."

"Your own?" the Marquis questioned. "I think, my precious one, that I shall have a part in them."

Lara blushed again, but she went on:

"I was thinking today, before you came, that I could . . . never have . . . any since I could never . . . marry anyone whom I did not . . . love as I love you."

The Marquis did not answer her but turned her face up to his and kissed her.

Because she realised she had excited him by what she had said, there was a fire on his lips which had not been there before and a passion that was very demanding.

It told her, without words, that he wanted her to surrender herself to him completely.

She knew as he kissed her and went on kissing her it was what she wanted too. She wanted to give him not only her heart and her soul but also her body.

"I want you," the Marquis said, and his voice was deep and hoarse. "How soon will you marry me?"

"I want to be . . . your wife," Lara answered. "I want it more than . . . anything else in the world. But I am still . . . afraid."

"Of me?" the Marquis asked.

She smiled.

"Not really, although you are frightening at times, but of being your wife . . . in case I . . . fail you."

"You will never do that," the Marquis replied. "I have a feeling, my darling, that the future is going to be an exciting adventure for both of us. We have

176

to discover a great deal about each other and for me it will be one of the most thrilling things I have ever done."

"Do you really mean that?" Lara questioned. "For if I felt that you would become cynical, bored, or contemptuous of me . . . after we had been married for a little while, it would be . . . better for me.to say no now rather than to . . . suffer the . . . agonies of Hell . . . later."

The Marquis's arms were like steel and it was hard for her to breathe as he said:

"I am not allowing you to say no. You are going to marry me just as soon as your father will perform the ceremony, and then I will have no time to be cynical when you will doubtlessly argue with me and nag me into doing a million things that I have never done before."

Lara laughed but he took the laughter from her lips with another kiss.

Then, as he held her captive, she knew that, while they would certainly argue and perhaps sometimes fight each other, their love was so great that it was, though he had not said so, different from any love the Marquis had known before.

This was not only the burning heat of the sun which made them desire each other as a man and a woman but also the spiritual white light of the moon which elevated their souls.

Together they would seek all that was highest and best and which like a prayer would carry them up to the sky.

Lara knew they had found together the love that she had been trying to express in her book, which she had seen in the beauty of the Priory and heard in the music she had played to Georgina.

It was the love that all men and women had sought down the ages.

It could never be complete in a man and woman separately, but must belong to both when, joined by the Sacrament of Marriage, they become one.

"I love ... you," Lara murmured against the Marquis's lips.

"I adore and worship you," he answered.

Then there was only the light of God to inspire, guide, and protect them, all through their lives together.

In 1976 by writing twenty-one books, she broke the world record and has continued for the following four years with twenty-four, twenty, twenty-three and twenty-four. She is in the *Guinness Book of Records* as the best selling author in the world.

She is unique in that she was one and two in the Dalton List of Best Sellers, and one week had four books in the top twenty.

In private life Barbara Cartland, who is a Dame of the Order of St. John of Jerusalem, Chairman of the St. John Council in Hertfordshire and Deputy President of the St. John Ambulance Brigade, has also fought for better conditions and salaries for Midwives and Nurses.

Barbara Cartland is deeply interested in Vitamin Therapy and is President of the British National Association for Health. Her book *The Magic of Honey* has sold throughout the world and is translated into many languages. Her designs "Decorating with Love" are being sold all over the USA and the National Home Fashions League named her in 1981, "Woman of Achievement."

Camfield Romances by

BARBARA CARTLAND

Called after her own beloved Camfield Place, each Camfield Romance by Barbara Cartland is a thrilling, never-before published love story by the greatest romance writer of all time!

February...THE POOR GOVERNESS
April...WINGED VICTORY
June...LUCKY IN LOVE

Watch for them!

SK-40